Hester Lilly

AND TWELVE SHORT STORIES

Hester Lilly

AND TWELVE SHORT STORIES

by Elizabeth Taylor

Short Story Index Reprint Series

BOOKS FOR LIBRARIES PRESS
FREEPORT, NEW YORK

Reprinted 1972 by arrangement with
The Viking Press, Inc.

Grateful acknowledgment is made to *The New Yorker*, which published "The Beginning of a Story," "The First Death of Her Life," "The Idea of Age," "Oasis of Gaiety," "A Red-Letter Day," "Spry Old Character," and "Swan-Moving,"; to *Harper's Magazine*, in which "The Light of Day" and "A Sad Garden" appeared; and to *Harper's Bazaar*, which published "I Live in a World of Make-Believe."

INTERNATIONAL STANDARD BOOK NUMBER:
0-8369-4137-3

LIBRARY OF CONGRESS CATALOG CARD NUMBER:
78-38724

PRINTED IN THE UNITED STATES OF AMERICA
BY
NEW WORLD BOOK MANUFACTURING CO., INC.
HALLANDALE, FLORIDA 33009

To Joanna and Renny

Contents

Hester Lilly

Hester Lilly

Muriel's first sensation was one of derisive relief. The name, Hester Lilly, had suggested to her a goitrous, pre-Raphaelite frailty. That, allied with youth, can in its touchingness spell danger to any wife, demanding protectiveness and chivalry, those least combatable adversaries, against which admiration simply is nothing. For if she is to fling herself on his compassion, Muriel had thought—at that age, and orphaned; then any remonstrance from me will seem doubly callous.

As soon as she saw the girl an injudicious confidence stilled her doubts. Her husband's letters from and to this young cousin seemed now fairly guiltless and untormenting—avuncular, but not in a threatening way.

Hester, in clothes which astonished by their improvisation—the wedding of outgrown school uniform with the adult, gloomy wardrobe of her dead mother—looked jaunty, defiant, and absurd. Every garment was grown out of or not grown into.

I will take her under my wing, Muriel promised herself. The idea of an unformed personality to be moulded and highlighted invigorated her, and the desire to tamper with —as in those fashion magazines in which ugly duckling is so disastrously changed to swan before our wistful eyes—made her impulsive and welcoming. She came quickly across the hall and laid her cheek against the girl's, murmuring affectionately. Deception enveloped them.

Robert was not deceived. He understood his wife's relief, and, glimpsing that, glimpsed the wary distress she must for some time have suffered. Now she was in command again, and her misgivings were gone. He also sensed that if at this point she was ceasing to suspect him, perhaps his own guilt was only just beginning. He hated the transparency of Muriel's sudden relaxation and forbearance. Until now she had contested his decision to bring Hester into their home, incredulous that she could not have her own way. She had laid about him with every weapon she could find—cool scorn, sweet reasonableness, little-girl tears.

"You are making a bugbear of her," he had said.

"*You* have made *her* that to *me*. For months all these letters going to and fro, sometimes three a week from her—and I always excluded."

She had tried not to watch him reading them, had poured out more coffee, re-examined her own letters. He always opened Hester's last of all and as if he would rather have read it privately. Then he would fold it and slip it back inside the envelope to protect it from her eyes. All round his plate, on the floor, were other screwed-up envelopes which had contained his less secret letters. Once, to break a silence, he had lied, said, "Hester sends love to you." In fact Hester had never written or spoken Muriel's name. Hers had not been family letters to be passed from one to the other, not cousinly letters with banal inquiries and remembrances. The envelopes had been stuffed with adolescent despair, cries of true loneliness; were repellent with egotism and affected bitterness, appealing with naïveté. Hester had been making, in this year since her father's death, a great hollow nest in preparation for love, and Robert had watched her going round and round it, brooding over it, covering it. Now it was ready and was empty.

Unknowingly, but with so many phrases in her letters, she had acquainted him with this preparation, which must be hidden from her mother and from Muriel. She had not imagined the letters as being read by anyone but Robert, and he would not betray her.

"You are old enough to be her father," Muriel had once said; but those scornful, recriminating, wife's words never sear and wither as they are meant to. They presented him instead with his first surprised elation. After that he looked forward to the letters and was disappointed on mornings when there were none.

If there were any guilty love, he was the only guilty one. Hester proceeded in innocence—wrote the letters blindly, as if to herself or as in a diary, and loved only men in books, or older women. She felt melancholy yearnings in cinemas and at the time of leaving home had become obsessed by a young pianist who played teatime music in a café.

Now at last, at the end of her journey, she felt terror, and as the first ingratiating smile faded from her face she looked sulky and wary. Following Muriel upstairs and followed by Robert carrying some of her luggage, she was overcome by the reality of the house, which she had imagined wrong. It was her first visit, and she had from Robert's letters constructed a completely different setting. Stairs led up from the side of the hall instead of from the end facing the door. "I must finish this letter and go up to bed," Robert had sometimes written. So he had gone up *these* stairs, she thought in bewilderment as she climbed them now.

The building might not have been a school. The mullioned windows had views of shaved lawns—deserted—and cedar trees.

"I thought there would be goalposts everywhere," she said, stopping at a landing window.

"In summertime?" Muriel asked in a voice of sweet amusement.

They turned into a corridor, and Robert showed Hester from another window the scene she had imagined. Below a terrace, a cinder track encircled a cricket field where boys were playing. A white-painted pavilion and sight-screens completed the setting. The drowsy afternoon quiet was broken abruptly by a bell's ringing, and at once voices were raised all over the building and doors were slammed.

When Muriel had left her—with many kind reminders and assurances—Hester was glad to be still for a moment and let the school sounds become familiar. She was pleased to hear them, for it was because of the school that she had come. She was not to share Muriel's life, whatever that might be, but Robert's. The social-family existence the three of them must lead would have appalled her if she had not known that after most mealtimes, however tricky, she and Robert would leave Muriel. They would go to his study, where she would prove, *must* prove, her efficiency—she had indeed knelt down for nights to pray that her shorthand would keep up with his dictation.

From the secretarial school where, aged eighteen, she had vaguely gone, she had often played truant. She had sat in the public gardens rather than face those fifteen-year-olds with their sharp ways, their suspicion of her, that she might from reasons of age or education think herself their superior. Her aloofness had been humble and painful, which they were not to know.

When Robert's offer had arrived she had regretted her time wasted. At her mother's death she was seen clearly to be the kind of girl whom relatives must help, take under their roof as governess or companion, or to do, as in Hester's case, some kind of secretarial work.

In spite of resentment, Muriel had given her a pleasant room, nicely anonymous, ready to receive the imprint of a long stay—no books, one picture, and a goblet of moss-roses.

Outside a gardener was mowing the lawn. There, at the back of the house, the lawns sloped up to the foot of a tree-covered hillside scarred by ravines. Foliage was dense and lush, banking up so that no sky was seen. Leaves were large enough to seem sinister, and all of this landscape with its tortured-looking ash trees, its too-prolific vegetation, had a brooding, an evil aspect—might have been a Victorian engraving, the end-piece to an idyllic chapter, hitting inadvertently, because of medium, quite the wrong note.

At the foot of the hillside, with lawns up to its porch, was a little church, which Hester knew from Robert's letters to be Saxon. Since the eighteenth century it had been used as a private chapel by the successive owners of the house—the last of these now impoverished and departed. The family graves lay under the wall. Once Robert had written that he had discovered an adder's nest there. His letters often—too often for Hester—consisted of nature notes, meticulously detailed.

Hester found this view from her window much more pre-envisaged than the rest. It had a strength and interest which her cousin's letters had managed to impart.

From the church—now used as school chapel—a wheezy, elephantine voluntary began, and a procession of choir boys, their royal-blue skirts trailing the grass or hitched up unevenly above their boots, came out of the house and paced, with a pace so slow they rocked and swayed, towards the church door. The chaplain followed, head bent, sleeves flung back on his folded arms. He was, as Hester already knew, a thorn in Robert's flesh.

In the drawing room Muriel was pouring out tea. Robert always stood up to drink his. It was a woman's hour, he felt, and his dropping in on it was fleeting and accidental. Hugh Baseden stood up as well—though wondering why—until Muriel said, "Won't you sit down, Mr. Baseden?"

At once he searched for reproof in her tone and thought that perhaps he had been imitating a piece of headmasterliness—not for him. Holding his cup unsteadily in one hand, he jerked up the knees of his trousers with the other and lowered himself onto the too-deep sofa, perched there on the edge, staring at the tea in his saucer.

Muriel had little patience with gaucherie, though inspiring it. She pushed aside Hester's clean cup and clasped her hands in her lap.

"What can she be doing?" she asked.

"Perhaps afraid to come down," Robert said.

Hugh looked with embarrassment at the half-open door

where Hester hesitated, peering in, clearly wondering if this were the right room and the right people in it. To give warning to the others, he stood up quickly and slopped some more tea into his saucer. Robert and Muriel turned their heads.

"We were thinking you must be lost," Muriel said, unsure of how much Hester may have heard.

Robert went forward and led her into the room. "This is Hugh Baseden. My cousin, Hester Lilly, Hugh. You are newcomers together, Hester, for this is Hugh's first term with us."

Hester sank down on the sofa, her knees at an inelegant angle. When asked if she would have sugar she said, "Yes," in error, and knew at once that however long her stay might be she was condemned to sweet tea throughout it; for she would never find the courage to explain.

"Mr. Baseden is one of those ghoulish schoolmasters who cut up dead frogs and put pieces of bad meat under glass to watch what happens," Muriel said. "I am sure it teaches the boys something enormously important, although it sounds so unenticing."

"Do girls not learn biology, then?" Hugh asked, looking from one to the other.

Muriel said, "No," and Hester said, "Yes"; and they spoke together.

"Then that is how much it has all changed," Muriel added lightly. "That marks the great difference in our ages"—she smiled at Hester—"as so much else does, alas! But I am glad I was spared the experience. The smell!" She put her hand delicately to her face and closed her eyes. Hester felt that the lessons she had learned had made her repulsive herself. "Oh, do you remember, Robert," Muriel went on, "last Parents' Day? The rabbit? I walked into the Science Room with

Mrs. Carmichael, and there it was, opened out, pinned to a board, and all its insides labelled. How we scurried off! All the mammas looking at their sons with awe and anxiety and fanning themselves with their handkerchiefs, wondering if their darlings would not pick up some plague. We must not have that this year, Mr. Baseden. You must promise me not. A thundery day—oh, by four o'clock! Could we have things in jars instead, sealed up? Or skeletons? I like it best when the little ones just collect fossils or flint arrowheads."

"Flint arrowheads are not in Hugh's department," Robert said; although Muriel knew that as well as he, was merely going through her scatterbrain performance—the all-feminine, inaccurate, negligent act by which she dissociated herself from the school.

"They are out of chapel," Hugh said. The noise outside was his signal to go. "No rabbits, then," he promised Muriel and, turning to Hester, said, "Don't be too bewildered. I haven't had much start on you, but I begin to feel at home." Then, sensing some rudeness to Muriel in what he had said, he added, "So many boys must be a great strain to you at first. You will get used to them in time."

"I never have," Muriel murmured when he had gone. "Such dull young men we get here always. I am sorry, Hester, there is no brighter company for you. Of course there is Rex Wigmore, ex-RAF, with moustache, slang, silk mufflers, undimmed gaiety; but I should be wary of him if I were you. You think I am being indiscreet, Robert; but I am sure Hester will know without being told how important it is in a school for us to be able to speak frankly—even scandalously —when we are *en famille*. It would be impossible to laugh if, outside, our lips were not sealed tight."

If everything is to be said for me, Hester thought, and understood for me, how am I ever to take part in a conversation again?

From that time Muriel spoke on her behalf, interpreted for her, as if she were a savage or a mute, until the moment, not many days later, when she told Hester in her amused but matter-of-fact voice, "Of course you are in love with Robert."

Muriel saved her the pains of groping towards this fact. She presented it promptly, fresh, illicit, and out-of-the-question; faced and decided once for all. The girl's heart swerved in horrified recognition. From her sensations of love for and dependence upon this older man, her cousin, she had separated the trembling ardour of her youth and unconsciously had directed it towards the less forbidden—the pianist in the café, for instance. Now she saw that her feelings about that young man were just the measure of her guilt about Robert.

Muriel insinuated the idea into the girl's head, thinking that such an idea would come sooner or later and came better from her, inseparable from the very beginning from shame and confusion. She struck, with that stunning remark, at the right time. For the first week or so Hester was tense with desire to please, anxiety that she might not earn her keep. Robert would often find her bowed in misery over indecipherable shorthand, or would hear her rip pages out of the typewriter and begin again. The wastepaper basket was usually crammed full of spoiled stationery. Once he discovered her in tears, and, when he was halfway across the room to comfort her, wariness overtook him. He walked instead to the window and spoke with his back to her, which seemed to him to be the only alternative to embracing her.

Twice before he had taken her in his arms, on two of the three times they had been together. He had met her when she came home from Singapore where her father had died, and she had begun to cry in the station refreshment room while they were having a cup of tea. His earlier meeting was at her christening, when he had dutifully, as godfather, held her for a moment. The third encounter she had inveigled him into. He had met her in London secretly to discuss an important matter. They had had luncheon at his club, and the important matter turned out to be the story of her misery at living with her mother—the moods, scenes, words, tears. He could see that she found telling him more difficult than she had planned—found it in fact almost impossible. Rehearsing her speeches alone, she had reckoned without his presence, his looks of embarrassment, the sound of her own voice complaining, her fear of his impatience. She had spoken in a high, affected, hurried voice, smiling too much and at the wrong moments, with a mixture of defiance and ingratiation he found irritating but pathetic. He had had so little solace to offer, except that he was sure the trouble would pass, that perhaps her mother suffered too, at the crisis of middle age. At that Hester had been overcome by a great, glowering blush, as if he had said something unforgivable. He did not know if it were some adolescent prudery in her, or the outrage of having excuses made for her enemy-mother—for whom excuses might have been made, for she died not long after, of cancer.

Now, as he stood at the window, listening to her tears, he knew that she was collapsed, abandoned, in readiness for his embrace of consolation, and he would not turn round, although his instinct was to go to her.

He said absurdly, "I hope you are happy here," and received of course only tears in answer.

Without physical contact he could not see how to bring the scene to an end. Bored, he surveyed the garden and thought that the box hedge needed trimming. Beyond this hedge, hanging from the branches of fruit trees, were old potatoes stuck with goosefeathers. He watched them twirling gaily above the currant bushes, not frightening the birds but exciting or bemusing them.

She realized that he would not come to her, and her weeping sank into muffled apologies, over which Robert could feel more authoritative, with something reassuring to say in return and something to do. (He fetched a decanter of sherry.) His reassurances were grave, not brusque. He put the reasons for her distress sensibly back upon legitimate causes, where perhaps they belonged—the death of her mother, shock, strain, fatigue.

He sat by his desk and put on his half-moon reading glasses, peered over them, swung about in his swivel chair, protecting himself by his best old-fogy act. "Muriel and I only want to make you happy."

Hester flinched.

"You must never let this work worry you, you know." He almost offered to get someone else to do it for her, his sense of pity was so great.

His reading glasses were wasted on her. She would not look at him with her swollen eyes, but pointed her hands together over her forehead, making an eave to hide her face.

"But does Muriel *want* me here?" she cried at last.

"Could you be here if she did not?"

"But do you?"

In her desperation she felt that she could ask any questions. The only advice he ever wanted to give young people was not to press desperation too far, uncreative as it is—*not* to admit recklessness. Muriel had once made similar mistakes. It seemed to him a great fault in women.

"I shall only mind having you here if you cry any more—or grow any thinner."

He glanced down at his feet. She was not really any thinner, but Muriel had begun work on her clothes, which now fitted her and showed her small waist and long narrow back.

"You are bound to feel awkward at first with each other," Robert said. "It is a strange situation for you both, and Muriel is rather shy."

Hester thought that she was uncouth and sarcastic—but not shy, not for one moment shy.

"I think she is trying so hard to be kind and sympathetic," he continued, "but she must make her own place in your life. She would not be so impertinent as to try to be a mother to you, as many less sensitive women might. There is no precedent to help her—having no children herself, being much older. She has her own friends, her own life, and she would like to make a place for you too. I think she would have loved to have a daughter—I can imagine that from the interest she takes in your clothes, for instance." This was true, had puzzled Hester, and now was made to shame her.

Muriel opened the door suddenly upon this scene of tears and sherry. Hester, to hide her face, turned aside and put up a hand to smooth her hair.

"Miss Graveney's address," Muriel said. She stood stiffly in front of Robert's desk while he searched through a file. She did not glance at Hester and held her hand out to take the address from Robert before he could bring it from the drawer. "Thank you, dear!" She spoke in her delicately amused voice, nodded slightly, and left the room.

Outside she began to tremble violently. Misery split her in two—one Muriel going upstairs in fear and anger, and another Muriel going beside her, whispering, "Quiet! Be calm. Think later."

Hester, with her new trimness, was less touching. She lost part of the appeal of youth—the advantage Muriel could not challenge—and won instead an uncertain sophistication, an unstable elegance, which only underlined how much cleverer Muriel was at the same game.

Muriel's cleverness, however, could not overcome the pain she felt. She held the reins but could barely keep her hands from trembling. Her patience was formidable. Robert had always remarked upon it since the day he had watched her at work upon her own wedding cake. There were many things in her life which no one could do as well as she, and her wedding cake was one of them. She had spent hours at the icing, at hair-fine latticework, at roses and rosettes, swags and garlands, conch shells and cornucopias. She had made of it a great work of art, and with a similar industry, which Robert only half discerned and Hester did not discern at all, she now worked at what seemed to her the battle for her marriage.

Conceived at the moment of meeting Hester, the strategy was based on implanting in the girl her own—Muriel's—

standards, so that every success that Hester had would seem one in the image of the older woman, and every action bring Muriel herself to mind. Patience, tolerance, coolness, amusement were parts of the plan, and when she suddenly said, "Of course you are in love with Robert," she had waited to say it for days. It was no abrupt cry of exasperation, but a piece of the design she had worked out.

Before Hester could reply, Muriel stressed the triviality of such a love by going on at once to other things. "If I were a young girl again I should have a dark dress made, like a Bluecoat Boy's—a high neck and buttoned front, leather belt, huge, boyish pockets hidden somewhere in the skirt. How nice if one could wear yellow stockings too!"

She rested her hand on her tapestry-frame and forced herself to meet Hester's eyes, her own eyes veiled and narrowed, as if she were considering how the girl would look in such a dress.

Hester's glance, as so often in the innocent party, wavered first. She had no occupation to help her, and stared down at her clasped hands.

Muriel began once more to pass the needle through the canvas. Diligently, week by week, the tapestry roses blossomed in grey and white and blood-colour.

"Don't you think?" she asked.

She swung the frame round and examined the back of the canvas. It was perfectly neat. She sat sideways in her chair with the frame-stand drawn up at an angle. Her full skirt touched the carpet—pink on crimson.

"Why do you say that?" Hester asked. "What makes you say it?" She sounded as if she might faint.

"Say what?"

"About Robert." Her lips moved clumsily over the name as if they were stung by it and swollen.

"Robert? Oh, yes! Don't fuss, dear girl. At your age one has to be in love with someone, and Robert does very well for the time being. Perhaps at *every* age one has to be in love with someone, but when one is young it is difficult to decide whom. Later one becomes more stable. I fell in love with all sorts of unsuitable people—very worrying for one's mother. By the time I met Robert I was old enough to be sure that *that* would last. As it has," she added quietly; and she chose a strand of white silk and began to work on the highlights of a rose petal.

"I once fell in love with a young man who drank like a fish," she continued, for Hester seemed stunned into silence. "He was really an evil influence—very flashy. You remember how I warned you about Rex Wigmore your first day here?" She began to shake with mirth. "Trying to be my own anxious mamma all over again! And all the time it was Robert! How lucky! For Robert is so gentle, so kind. He would never harm you. Nothing but good could come of a girl loving *him*. Yes, I can see Robert doing very well indeed, until the real one comes along. How furious he would be to hear us discussing him like this; men take themselves so seriously."

"I am not discussing him," Hester said, an ugly stubbornness in her manner. She snatched a handkerchief from her pocket and began to fidget with it, crushing it and smoothing it and staring at it in a bewildered defiance.

Muriel's white hand smoothed a woollen rose. "I always leave the background till last." She sighed. "So dull, going on and on with the same colour."

"It isn't true. He's my cousin, much older, your husband —I—does he know?"

"Well, I haven't asked him. Men are too vain. I daresay he knows all right, though. It's very good for them, at his age—makes them feel young."

So Hester saw herself thrust into the service of nature, a coarse instrument, as good as anonymous. Muriel, spared such humiliation, could well smile and congratulate herself. "Don't fuss," she said again in her most laughing voice. "If I had known you would, I wouldn't have said it."

"I wish I could go away." Hester wrung her hands and looked towards the windows as if she might escape through them. "You hate me being here. And now—"

"Now?"

"Now you believe this about me, how can you bear me to be here? No wife could."

At this a stern, fastidious look came upon Muriel's face. She was silent for a moment, then said in a quiet and serious voice, "I—as a wife; Robert—as a husband; our private life together I must leave out of this. It is between us only, and I never discuss my marriage."

"There is no need to be rude to me," Hester shouted, so great her frustration, so helplessly she felt herself up against Muriel's smooth contempt. She was forced into childishness.

At her outburst—for all of today was working for Muriel, she thought—the door opened.

"But surely there is nothing sinister in that?" Beatrice Carpenter asked. She was Muriel's closest friend, and they were walking in the park before dinner. "Young girls often cry. You rather surprise me, Muriel. You sound hysterical yourself."

"It was the atmosphere of the room. It trembled with apprehension, and when I opened the door Robert looked at me with a dumbfounded expression, his eyes opened wide over those awful half-moon glasses he *will* wear; they—his eyes—looked so *blue*—a little boy's look, little boy in mischief. 'Don't spank me, Nannie.' I hated him for a moment. Oh, I felt murderous. No, but I truly itched to hurt him physically, by some violent and abusive act, to hit him across the mouth, to—" She broke off in astonishment and looked about her, as if fearful of being overheard.

"You *are* in a bad way," Beatrice said. "The girl will have to go."

"I know. But how? I have to be clever, not insistent. I can't be put into the position of getting my own way, for it would never be forgotten. It would last all our lives, such a capitulation, you know."

Other married women *always* know, so Beatrice only murmured cosily.

Muriel said, "The self-consciousness is so deadly. When I go back he will look at me to see how I am likely to behave. Every time I go into a room he glances at my face, so that I can no longer meet his eyes."

"I never think embarrassment is a trivial emotion," Beatrice said.

"It has altered everything, having her here; for we were just at an age of being able, perhaps, to relax, to take each other for granted, to let ourselves slip a little. It is a compensation for growing old, and one must find a compensation for that if one can."

"I cannot," Beatrice said.

"For a day or two I tried to compete, but I will not be forced into the sort of competition I am bound to lose." Muriel frowned and with a weary gesture unclipped her gold earrings as if she suddenly found their weight intolerable. She walked on with them clutched, warm and heavy, in her hand. Beatrice could not bear the sight of her fiery earlobes. She was upset by that, as when people who always wear glasses take them off for polishing and expose their wounded-looking and naked eyes. Muriel was never without earrings and might have caused slightly less concern by suddenly unpinning her hair.

Beatrice said, "An experienced woman is always held to be a match for a young girl, but I shouldn't like to have to try it. Not that I *am* very experienced."

They sat down on a seat under a rhododendron bush, for now they were in the avenue leading to the house, and their conversation had not neared its end, as their walk had.

By "experience" both meant love affairs. Beatrice thought of the engagement she had broken in girlhood, and Muriel thought of Hugh Baseden's predecessor and his admiration for her, which she had rather too easily kept within bounds. It was, as Beatrice had said, very little experience, and had served no useful purpose and taught them nothing.

"And then," Muriel said, "there is the question of the marriage-bed." She was dropping the earrings from one hand to the other in her agitation. Far from never discussing her marriage, as she had assured Hester, she was not averse to going over it in every detail, and Beatrice was already initiated into its secrets to an extent which would have dismayed Robert had he known. "There were always so many wonderful excuses, or if none came to mind one could fall inextricably into a deep sleep. He has really been fairly mild and undemanding."

"Unlike Bertie," Beatrice said, and her sigh was genuinely regretful.

"Now I am afraid to make excuses or fall asleep. I scent danger and give in. That may seem obvious too. It is very humiliating. And certainly a bore."

"I sometimes pretend it is someone else," Beatrice said. "That makes it more amusing." She covered her face with her hands, bowed down, rocking with laughter at some incongruous recollection. "The most improbable men—if they could know!"

"But you might laugh at the time," Muriel said in an interested voice.

"I do—oh, I do."

"Robert would be angry."

"Perhaps husbands sometimes do the same."

Muriel clipped her earrings back on. She was herself again. "Oh, no!" she said briskly. "It would be outrageous."

"Marriage-bed" was only one of her many formal phrases. She also thought and talked of "bestowing favours" and "renewed ardours." To no one else, she told herself firmly. To no one else. They walked on up the avenue in silence, Beatrice still trembling, dishevelled with laughter. To no one else? Muriel thought, in another of those waves of nausea she had felt of late.

As they went upstairs before dinner she felt an appalling heaviness. She clung to the banisters, and Beatrice's voice came to her from afar. Clouded, remote, and very cold, she sat down at her dressing table. Beatrice took up the glass paperweight, as she always did, and said, as she always said, "These forever fascinate me." She tipped it upside-down, and snow began to drift, then whirl, about the little central figure. Muriel watched, the comb too heavy to lift. She watched the figure—a skating lady with raised muff and Regency bonnet—solitary, like herself, blurred, frozen, imprisoned.

"Will she be at dinner?" Beatrice was asking. She flopped down on the marriage-bed itself, still playing with the paperweight.

Hester, at dinner, did not appear to Beatrice to be a worthy adversary to a woman of Muriel's elegance. She said nothing except when coaxed by Muriel herself into brief replies; for Muriel had acquired courage and was fluent and vivacious, making such a social occasion of the conversation that they seemed to be characters in a play. *This* is how experienced people behave, she seemed to imply. We never embarrass by breaking down. In society we are impervious.

Robert patronized their conversation in the way of husbands towards wives' women friends—a rather elaborate but absent-minded show of courtesy. When Hester spilled some wine he dipped his napkin into the water jug and sponged the tablecloth without allowing an interruption of what he was saying. He covered her confusion by a rather long speech, and at its end Hugh Baseden was ready to take over with an even longer speech of his own. This protectiveness on their part only exposed Hester the more, for Beatrice took the opportunity of not having to listen to observe the girl more closely. She also observed that clumsiness can have a kind of appeal she had never suspected.

She observed technically at first—the fair, thick hair which needed drastic shaping. It was bunched up with combs which looked more entangled than controlling. The face was set in an expression that was sulky yet capable of breaking into swift alarm—even terror—as when her hand had knocked against the wineglass. The hands themselves were huge and helpless—rough, reddened, the nails cropped down. A piece of dirty sticking-plaster covered one knuckle. A thin silver bracelet hung over each wrist.

Then Beatrice observed that Hugh Baseden's protectiveness was ignored, but that Robert's brought forth a flush and tremor. While he was sponging the tablecloth the girl watched his hand intently, as if it had a miraculous or terrifying power of its own. Not once did she look at his face.

Beatrice thought that an ominous chivalry hung in the air, and she could see that every victory Muriel won contributed subtly to her defeat. Muriel should try less, she decided. Beatrice was the only one who enjoyed her dinner.

The boys were all in from the fields and gardens before Robert and Muriel dined, but throughout the meal those in the dining room were conscious of the school life continuing behind the baize-covered doors. The sounds of footsteps in the tiled passages, and of voices calling, went on for a long time, and while coffee was being served the first few bars of "Marche Militaire" could be heard again and again—the same brisk beginning, and always the same tripping into chaos. Start afresh. Robert beat time with his foot. Muriel sighed. Soon she accompanied Beatrice out to her car, and at once Hester, rather than stay in the room with Robert (for Hugh Baseden had gone off to some duty), went up to her room.

Now a curious stillness had fallen over the school, a silence drawn down almost by force. The "Marche Militaire" was given up, and other sounds could be heard—Muriel saying good-bye to Beatrice out on the drive, and an owl crying, for the light was going.

Hester knelt by her window with her elbows on the sill. Evening after evening she thought thunder threatened, and because it did not come she had begun to wonder if the strange atmosphere was a permanent feature of this landscape and intensified by her own sense of foreboding. The black hillside trees, the grape-coloured light over the church, and the bilious green lawns were the after-dinner scene, and she longed for darkness to cover it.

Beatrice's car went down the long drive. A door banged. So Muriel had come in, had returned to the drawing room to be surprised at Hester's absence. That averted look which she assumed when she entered rooms where Robert and Hester were alone would have been wasted.

Hester leaned far out of the window. Only the poplars made any sound—a deep sigh and then a shivering and clattering of their leaves. The other trees held out their branches mutely, and she imagined them crowded with sleeping birds, and bright-eyed creatures around their holes, arching their backs, baring their teeth, and swaying their noses to and fro for the first scents of the night's hunting. Her suburban background with its tennis courts, laburnum trees, golden privet, had not taught her how to be brave about the country; she saw only its vice and frightfulness and remembered the adders in the churchyard and the lizards and grass-snakes which the boys collected. Fear met her at every turn—in her dealings with people, her terror of Muriel, her shrinking from nature, her anxiety about her future. ("You are scrupulously untidy," Robert had said. Only a relative would employ her, and she had none but him.)

She made spasmodic efforts to come to terms with these fears; but in trying to face Muriel she fell, she knew, into sullenness. Nature she had not yet braved, had not penetrated the dense woods or the lush meadows by the lake where the frogs were. This evening—as a beginning, and because nature was the least of her new terrors, and from loneliness, panic, despair—she moved away from the window, stumbling on her cramped legs, and then went as quietly as she could downstairs and out of doors.

In the garden, at each rustle in the undergrowth, her ankles weakened, but she walked on, treading carefully on the dew-soaked grass. A hedgehog zigzagged swiftly across her path and checked her. She persisted, hoping thus to restore a little of her self-respect. She was conscious that each pace was taking her from her safe room, where nothing made her recoil but that phrase of Muriel that she carried everywhere—"Of course you are in love with Robert." It was better when we wrote the letters, she thought. I was happy then—I believe.

As the severest test she set herself the task of walking through the churchyard, where a mist hung over gravestones and nettles. The sound of metal striking flint checked her, and more normal fears than fears of nature came to her almost as a relief, as even burglars might be welcomed in an excessively haunted house. The dusk made it difficult

for her to discern what kind of figure was kneeling beside a headstone under the church walls; but as she stepped softly forward across the turf she could see it was an old lady in black flowing clothes and a straw garden-hat swathed with black ribbon. She wore gardening gloves and was planting out salvias and marguerites.

Hester tripped and grazed her arm against some granite. At her cry of pain the old lady looked up.

"Oh, mercy!" she exclaimed, holding the trowel to her heart. "For pity's sake, girl, what are you doing?"

Her white face was violin-shaped, narrowing under her cheekbones, and then widening again, but less, on the level of her wide, thin, lavender-coloured lips. The sagging cords of her throat were drawn in by a black velvet ribbon.

"I was only going for a walk," said Hester.

"I should call it prowling about. Have you an assignation here? With one of those schoolmasters from the house?"

"No."

The old lady drove the trowel into the earth, threw out stones, then, shaking another plant from a pot, wedged it into the hole. The grave resembled a bed in a public garden, with a neat pattern of annuals. The salvias bled hideously over a border of lobelias and alyssum. Their red was especially menacing in the dusky light.

"I think a grave should have *formality*," the old lady said as if she knew Hester's thoughts and was correcting them. " 'Keep it neat, and leave it at that,' I warned myself when my father died. I longed to express myself in rather unusual ways; my imagination ran riot with azaleas. A grave is no place for self-expression, though; no place for the indulgence of one's own likings. These flowers are not to my taste at all; they are in *no* taste."

"Is this your father's grave, then?" Hester asked.

"Yes." The old lady pointed with her trowel. "The one you are lolling against is grandfather's. Mother chained off over there with my sister, Linda. She did not want to go in with father. I can never remember them sharing a bed, even."

Hester, removing her elbow from the headstone, peered at the name. "Then you lived in the house?" she asked. "This name is carved over the stables."

"Our home before Domesday—three houses, at least, on this site, and brasses in the church going back to the Crusades. Now there are only the graves left—the name going too. For there were only Linda and I. Families decline more suddenly than they can rise. Extraordinarily interesting. The collapse of a family is most dramatic—I saw it all happen. The money goes, no sons are born—just daughters, and sometimes they arc not quite the thing. My sister Linda was weak in the head. We did have to pinch and scrape, and aunts fastened to us like barnacles on a wreck. Some of them drank, and the servants followed their example. Then tradespeople become insolent, although the *nouveau riche* still fawn." She turned up a green penny with her trowel, rubbed dirt from it, and put it in her pocket. "Our disintegration was fairly rapid," she said. "I *can* remember a time before it all overtook us—the scandals and gossip, threadbare carpets, dented silver, *sold* silver, darned linen. Oh, it usually goes the same way for everyone, once it begins. And very fascinating it can be—dry rot, wood-worm, the walls subsiding; cracks in plaster *and* in character. Even the stonework in the house has some sort of insect in it." She nodded proudly at the school. "Unless they have done something about it."

"Do you come here often?"

"Yes. Yes, I do. I tend the graves. It makes an outing. I once went to the school to have tea with Mrs. Thingummy—a nice little woman." This, Hester supposed, was Muriel. "Interesting to see what they made of it. I liked the school part very much. I went all over, opened every door. I thought the chance might not come again. Into the servants' wing, where I had never been before—very nice dormitories and bathrooms. The bathrooms were splendid—little pink, naked boys splashing under showers, a very gay and charming sight, I could hardly drag myself away. They scuttled off as shy as crabs. I expect the look of me startled them. What I did *not* admire was the way she had managed the private part of the house where we had tea—loose covers, which I abhor. I thought it all showed a cool disregard for the painted ceiling. Never mind, I satisfied my curiosity, and no need to be bothered with her again."

Hester, though feeling that Muriel might in fairness be allowed to furnish her drawing room as she pleased, was none the less delighted to hear this censure, especially over matters of taste. She longed to talk more of Muriel, for she had no other confidante, and this old lady, though strange, was vigorous in her scorn and might, if she were encouraged, say very much more.

"I live there now," she began.

In the darkness, which she had hardly noticed, the old lady had begun to stack up her empty flowerpots.

"Then you will be able to do me a small favour," she said,

"in connection with the graves. If it fails to rain tonight I should be obliged if you would water these plants for me in the morning—a good sousing before the sun gets strong."

She pulled herself to a standing position with one hand on the gravestone. Her joints snapped with a frail and brittle sound as she moved. Hester faced her across the grave and faced too the winy, camphorous smell of her breath and her clothes.

"Only Father's grave. I shall plant Mother's and Linda's tomorrow evening."

She swayed, steadying herself against the stone and then, with a swinging movement as if on deck in wild weather, made off through the churchyard, lurching from one gravestone to another, her hands out to balance her, her basket swinging from her arm. She was soon lost to Hester's sight, but the sound of her unsteady progress as she brushed through branches of yew and scuffled the gravel continued longer. When she could hear no more the girl walked back to the house. She had forgotten the snakes and the bats and all the terrors of nature; and she found that for a little while she had forgotten Robert, and Muriel too, and the sorrows and shame of love.

As she crossed the lawn Hugh Baseden and Rex Wigmore came round the house from the garages. Stepping out of the darkness into the light shed from upstairs windows, she looked pale-skinned and mysterious, and both men were arrested by a change in her. The breeze blew strands of hair forward across her face, and she turned her head impatiently so that the hair was whipped back again, lifting up from her ears, around which it hung so untidily by day.

"I thought you were a ghost coming from the churchyard," Hugh said. "Weren't you nervous out there by yourself?"

"No."

But her teeth began to chatter, and she drew her elbows tight to her waist to stop herself from shivering.

"What *have* you been up to?" Rex asked.

"I went for a walk."

"Alone? How absurd. How wasteful. How unsafe! You never know what might happen to you. If you want to go for a walk you could always ask me. I like being out with young girls in the dark. I make it even unsafer. And at least you could be quite sure what would happen to you then."

"You are cold," Hugh said. He opened the door and, as she stepped past him into the hall, brushed his hand down her bare arm. "You *are* cold."

Rex's remarks, which he deplored, had excited him. He imagined himself—not Rex—walking in the dark with her. He had had so few encounters with women, so few confidings, explorings; and longed to take on some hazards and excitements.

Rex, whose life was full enough of all those things, was bored and wandered off. He found her less attractive—hardly attractive at all—indoors and in the bright light of the hall.

Hester rarely spoke at mealtimes, but next morning at breakfast she mentioned the old lady.

"Miss Despenser." Muriel put her hand to her face as she had when speaking of the dead rabbit in the laboratory. She breathed as if she felt faint. "She came to tea once—once only. I wondered if I should pour whisky in her tea. She is the village drunk. I believe her sister was the village idiot—but now dead."

"You shouldn't go out late at night on your own," Robert said. "You might catch cold," he added, for he could really think of no reason why she should not go—only the vague unease we feel when people venture out late alone, a guilty sense of having driven them out, or of having proved inadequate to keep them or still their restlessness or win their confidence.

"It is a wonder she could spare time from the Hand and Flowers," Muriel said. "I am surprised to hear of her tidying the graves in licensed hours."

"And shall you water the plants?" Robert asked in amusement.

"I have done. She said before the sun got too strong."

"What impertinence!" Muriel said, and every lash at Miss Despenser was really one at Hester. She felt even more agitated and confused this morning, for Rex's words, with their innuendo and suggestion, had been spoken beneath her bedroom window the previous night, and she, lying in bed, half reading, had heard him.

Until that moment she had seen the threat in Hester's youth, defencelessness, and pathos; but she had not thought of her as being desirable in any more obvious way. Rex's words—automatic as they were, almost meaningless as they must be from him—proved that the girl might also be desirable in the most obvious way of all. Muriel's distaste and hostility were strengthened by what she had overheard. Still more, a confusion in herself, which she was honest enough to ponder, disquieted her. To be jealous of Hester where Robert was concerned was legitimate and fitting, she thought; but to be jealous of the girl's least success with other men revealed a harshness from which she turned sickly away. There was nothing now which she could allow Hester, no generosity or praise; grudged words of courtesy which convention forced her to speak seemed to wither on her lips with the enormity of their untruthfulness.

Her jealousy had grown from a fitful nagging to a chronic indisposition, an unreasonableness beyond her control.

She went, after breakfast, to her bedroom, without waiting to see Hester follow Robert to his study. The days had often seemed too long for her, and now pain had its own way of spinning them out. To go to her kitchen and begin some healing job like baking bread would have appeared to her cook as a derangement and a nuisance. She was childless, kitchenless, without remedy or relief.

Robert, she thought, had not so much become a stranger as revealed himself as the stranger he had for a long time been. The manifestation of this both alarmed her and stirred her conscience. Impossible longings which had sometimes unsettled her—especially in the half-seasons and at that hour when the light, beginning to fade, invests garden or darkening room with a romantic languor—had seemed a part of her femininity. The idea that men—or men like Robert—should be beset by the same dangerous sensations would have astonished her by its vulgarity. Their marriage had continued its discreet way. Now she could see how it had changed its course from those first years with their anniversaries, secrets, discussions, his hidden disappointment over her abortive pregnancies, the consolation and the bitter tears—all embarrassing now in her memory, but shouldering their way up through layers of discretion to wound and worry her. She had allowed herself to change; but she could tolerate no change in Robert, except for the decline in his ardour, which she had felt herself reasonable in expecting.

In rather the same spirit as Hester's when she had faced the terrors of the churchyard the night before, Muriel now went into Robert's dressing room and shut the door. She knelt down before a chest and, pulling out the bottom drawer, found, where she knew she would find them, among his old school photographs, the bundle of letters she had written to him when they were betrothed.

She felt nausea, but a morbid impatience, as if she were about to read letters from his mistress. The first of the pile began: "Dear Mr. Evans . . ." It was a cool but artful invitation. She remembered writing it after their first meeting, thinking he had gone forever and wanting to draw him back to her. "I am writing for my mother, as she is busy." Not only had he been drawn back, but he had kept the letter. Perhaps he had had his own plans for their meeting again. She might well have let things be and sat at home and waited—so difficult a thing for a young girl to do.

That first letter was the only time he was "Mr. Evans." After that he progressed from "Dear Robert" through "My Dear Robert," "Dearest Robert," "Robert Dearest," to "Darling." In the middle period of the letters—for he had preserved them chronologically—the style was comradely, witty, undemanding. (Intolerably affected, Muriel now thought, her neck reddening with indignation. Arch! Oh, yes!) Did Hester write so to him, and could he, at his age, feel no distaste? The letters, patently snobbish, shallow, worked up, had taken hours to write, she remembered. Everything that happened during the day was embroidered for Robert at night—the books she read were used only as a bridge between their two minds. The style was parenthetic, for she could not take leave even of a sentence. So many parentheses scattered about gave the look of her eyelashes having been shed upon the pages. When she had written "Yours, Muriel" or, later, "Your Muriel," there was always more to come, many postscripts to stave off saying good night. Loneliness, longing broke through again and again, despite the overlying insincerity. She had, writing in her room at night, so wanted Robert. Like a miracle, or as a result of intense concentration, she had got what she wanted. Kneeling before the drawer, with the letters in her hand, she was caught up once more in amazement at this fact. I got what I wanted, she thought over and over again.

His letters to her had often disappointed, especially in the later phase, when possessiveness and passion coloured her own. Writing so late at night, she had sometimes given relief to her loneliness. Those were momentary sensations, but his mistake had lain in taking them as such—in writing, in his reply, of quite other things. "But did you *get* my letter?" Muriel now read—the beginning of a long complaint which she was never to finish reading; for the door opened, and Robert was staring at her with an expression of aloof noncomprehension, as if he had suddenly been forced to close his mind at this intimation of her character.

Muriel said shakily, "I came across our old letters to each another—or rather mine to you. I could not resist them."

He still stared, but she would not look at him. Then he blinked, seemed to cast away some unpleasant thoughts, and said coldly, holding up a letter which she still would not glance at, "Lady Bewick is running this dance after the garden party. I came up to ask how many tickets we shall want."

"I thought you were taking Latin," Muriel said naïvely.

"They are having Break now." And indeed, if she had had ears to hear it, she would have known by the shouting outside.

"I should let her know today," Robert said. "Whom shall we take?"

Muriel was very still. Warily she envisaged the prospects: Hester going along too; Hester's brown, smooth shoulders dramatized by her chalk-white frock; Robert's glance at them; Muriel's pale, veined arms incompletely hidden by her lace stole. Perhaps Hester was a good dancer. Muriel herself was too stiff and rather inclined, from panic, to lead her partner.

"Why could we not go alone?" she asked.

"We could; but I thought we should be expected to take a party."

"Whom do you think?"

"I had no thoughts. I came to ask you."

"I see." He wants it every way, she thought—for her to go, and for me to suggest it. She tied up the letters and put them away.

"You should take Hester," she said suddenly. She began to tremble with anger and unhappiness. "I can stay at home."

"I had no intention of taking Hester."

"I suppose you are angry with me for reading those letters. I know it was wrong of me to open your drawer. I have never done such a thing in my life before." She still sat on the floor and seemed exhausted, keeping her head bent as she spoke.

"I can believe that. Why did you now?" he asked.

For a moment gentleness, the possibility of understanding, enveloped them; but she let it go, could think only of her suspicions, her wounded pride.

The tears almost fell, but she breathed steadily and they receded. "I was bored—not easy not to be. I remembered something—I was talking to Beatrice about it yesterday. I knew I should have written it somewhere in my letters to you. I was sure you wouldn't mind my looking." Her excuses broke off, and at last she dared to look at him. She smiled defiantly. "I wrote them, you know. You seem as cross as if they were written by another woman."

"They were," he said.

She was stunned. She slammed the drawer shut and stood up. She thought: Those are the worst words he ever spoke to me.

"I shall have to go," he said. "I suppose I can leave this till this afternoon." He held up the letter in his hand. "I didn't want to discuss it at lunch, that was all. The point is that Lady Bewick hoped we could take a partner for her niece, who is staying there—she thought we could ask one of the staff. I wondered if Hugh—"

"But he's so boring."

"We need not stay together."

"Take Rex."

"Rex?"

"Why not? He dances well."

"But he's so impossible. You have never disguised your scorn for him."

"He would be better than Hugh—not so achingly tedious." Irritability, the wish to sting, underlined her words. You are achingly tedious too, she seemed to imply. Her voice was higher-pitched than usual, her cheeks flushed. He looked at her in concern, then said, "All right. Three tickets, then." He put the letter in his pocket and turned away.

As soon as he had gone, but too late, she broke into weeping.

They dined at home before the dance. Muriel was intimidating but uncertain in too many diamonds. Her careless entrance into the drawing room had astonished Robert. She was shrugged up in a pink woollen shawl, through which came a frosty glitter. Rex's look of startled admiration confirmed her fear that she was overdressed. She has never erred in that way before, Robert thought. But she had shown several new faults of late; flaws had appeared which once he could not have suspected. There was, too, something slyly affected about the cosy shawl and the stir and flash of diamonds beneath it.

"It is only a countrified sort of dance," Robert told Rex. His words were chiefly for Muriel, who should have known. "Nothing very exciting. Good of you to turn out."

He hoped that Hester would now feel that she would miss nothing by staying at home, that he would not have gone himself, except as a duty, or asked anyone else to go, except as a favour. His stone, which should have killed two birds, missed both.

Hester, wearing a day frock and trying to look unconcerned, managed only a stubborn sullenness. A Cinderella performance, Muriel thought wrongly, underlined by Rex's greeting to the girl—"But you are coming with us, surely?"—when her clothes made it quite obvious that she was not.

Robert's shame, Muriel's guilt, Hester's embarrassment, seemed not to reach Rex, although for the other three the air shivered, the wineglasses trembled, at his tactlessness.

"Too bad," he said easily. "Well, there is no doubt that *you* are coming." He turned to Muriel, his eyes resting once more upon all her shimmering glitter. ("Ice," he called it, and later, to Hugh Baseden, "Rocks the size of conkers. Crown jewels. The family coffers scraped to the bottom.")

The glances that he had meant to appear gallant and flattering looked so predatory that Muriel put her hand to the necklace in a gesture of protection, and a bracelet fell into the soup. She laughed as Rex leaned forward and fished it out with a spoon and fork and dropped it into the napkin she held out. Her laughter was that simulated kind which is difficult to end naturally, and her eyes added to all the tremulous glint and shimmer of her. Hester, coldly regarding her, thought that she would cry. A Muriel in tears was a novel, horrifying idea.

The bracelet lay on the stained napkin. "The catch must be loose. I shan't wear it," Muriel said, and pushed it aside.

That will be one less, Robert thought.

After dinner he had a moment alone with Hester.

"All rather awkward about this dance. I hope you don't mind, my dear. Don't like leaving you—like Cinderella."

Hester could see Muriel, repowdered, cocooned in tulle, coming downstairs, and laughed at this illusion, remembering who did go to the ball in the fairy tale. "We must go to a real dance another time," Robert said. "Not a country hop, but a proper dance with buckets of champagne." But Muriel, rustling across the hall, finished this vision for them. "I should sit with Matron," he added.

"Oh, it is quite all right," Hester said with a brightness covering her extreme woundedness. "I could not have gone with you tonight, or sit with Matron either, because I have another engagement, and now I must hurry." With a glance at their halted expressions she ran upstairs, leaving behind an uneasiness and raised eyebrows.

The cistern in the downstairs cloakroom made a clanking sound, and there was a dreadful rush of water. This always embarrassed Muriel and she turned aside as Rex appeared.

Hester, at the bend of the stairs, called out in a ringing, careless voice, "Oh, do have a lovely time."

In this exhortation she managed to speak to them both in different ways—a difficult thing to do. Muriel felt herself condescended to and dismissed, unenvied, like a child going to a treat. But Robert's guilt was not one scrap appeased, and Hester did not mean it to be. He perceived both her pathos and her gallantry, as she desired. Her apparent lack of interest in their outing and her sudden look of excitement worried him. Even Rex was puzzled by her performance. *Now* what's she up to? he wondered as they went out to the car.

Yet, when she was in her own room, Hester could not imagine where she might go. Recklessness would have led her almost anywhere, but in the end she could think only of the churchyard. As Miss Despenser had said, "To water the graves makes an outing," and perhaps she could borrow a grave—Miss Linda's, for instance—and cherish it in such dull times as these.

When she arrived in the churchyard she found that Miss Despenser had finished planting and was vigorously scrubbing the headstones. Dirty water ran down over an inscription. "That's better," were her first words to Hester as she came near.

"I watered the plants."

"Yes, I noticed that."

"Can I help you?"

Miss Despenser threw the filthy water out in a great arc over some other graves—not her own family ones, Hester was sure—and handed her the bucket. "Clean water from the tap by the wall."

"Is that where the adders were?"

"Adders?"

"There were some once. I thought they might have come again."

"This is a fine thing, a stranger telling me about my own churchyard. I know nothing of adders. Are you a naturalist?"

"Oh, no! I am really rather afraid of nature."

Miss Despenser threw out her arms and laughed theatrically. "You're a damn witty girl, I know that. When I first met you I thought you were a bit of a nincompoop. You improve on acquaintance." She turned to examine the lettering on the grave, and Hester went to fetch the water.

"Afraid of nature!" Miss Despenser said when she returned. "I appreciate that."

The water, swinging in the pail, had slopped over into Hester's sandals, and her feet moved greasily in them.

"So you're afraid of nature!" Miss Despenser said, and she grasped the bucket and threw the water over the headstones. Some went over her, and more into Hester's sandals.

She is drunk, Hester thought, remembering Muriel's words and feeling annoyance that there should be any truth in them.

"The bucket goes back into the shed and the scrubbing brush into the basket." Miss Despenser shook drops of water off her skirt. "And we will go down to call on Mrs. Brimmer."

"Mrs. Brimmer?"

"A friend of mine. You are quite welcome. I will look in at the house first and leave the scrubbing brush. Mrs. Brimmer would think me rather eccentric if I went to see her with a scrubbing brush in my basket."

"Any adders?" she asked when Hester came back from the toolshed. The piquancy of her own humour delighted her, and she returned to the allusion again and again, puzzling Hester, who expected drunkenness to affect the limbs but not the wits and was exasperated, as the young so often are, at failing to read an extra meaning into the remarks of their elders.

Through a kissing-gate they came into a wood of fir trees. Miss Despenser slid and scuffled down the sloping track, which was slippery with pine needles. Jagged white flints had surfaced the path like the fins of sharks, so that Miss Despenser tripped and stumbled until Hester took her arm. She thought that they must look a strange pair and—such were the creaking darkness and mysterious resinous smell of the wood—half feared that as the path curved they might see themselves coming towards them through the trees, like a picture of Rosetti's she remembered called "How They Met Themselves." "I shouldn't care to meet myself," she said aloud, "in this dark place."

"You wouldn't recognize yourself. You are much too

young. When at long last you really learn what to look for, you will be too old to be alarmed."

"I didn't mean that I should or could—just that I'd hate it."

"I meet myself every so often. 'You hideous old baggage,' I say, and I nod. For years I thought it was someone else."

"This wood goes on and on," Hester said nervously.

"Ah, you are frightened of adders." When she had finished laughing Miss Despenser said, "When I go into the town to get the cat's meat, the chances are that as I go round by the boot shop I see myself walking towards me—in a long panel of mirror at the side of the shop. Horrid old character, I used to think; I must change my shopping morning. So I changed to Fridays, but there she was on Fridays just the same. 'I can't seem to avoid her,' I told myself. And no one can. Go on your holidays. You take yourself along too. Go to the ends of the earth—no escape. And one gets so bored, bored. I've had nearly seventy years of it now. And I wonder if, if I'd been beautiful or clever, I might have been less irritated. Perhaps I am difficult to please. My mother didn't care for *her*self either. When she died the vicar said, 'It is only another life she has gone to; an *everlasting* life.' An extraordinarily trite little man. He hadn't got much up here." She tapped her forehead and stumbled badly. "I said to him, 'Oh dear, oh dear, for pity's sake, hasn't she had enough of herself?' I asked. He couldn't answer that one. He just stared at the glass of sherry I was drinking, as if he were taking comfort in the idea of my being drunk. 'I believe in personality,' I said. 'You believe in souls. That's the difference between us.' Souls are flattened out, and one might very well spend an eternity with one's own—though goodness knows what it would be like, as interesting as a great bowl of nourishing soup. I always think of souls as saucers, full of some tepid, transparent liquid—couldn't haunt anyone. Personalities do the haunting—Papa's for instance. Tiresome, dreadful things. Can't shake them off. Unless under the influence, of course."

Of drink, I suppose, Hester thought.

"Of drink," the old lady added.

"It *is* a gruesome place. I like trees that shed their leaves."

The bark of the trees was blood-red in the dying light, and there were no sounds of birds or anything but branches creaking and tapping together. Then the pink light thinned, the trees opened out, and blueness broke through, and in this new light was a view of a tilted hillside with houses, and a train buffeting along through cornfields.

"And there is my home," Miss Despenser said. She scrambled down the bank into a lane, and, as she brushed dust and twigs from her skirt, she crossed the lane and opened a gate.

Laurels almost barred the way to the little house, which was of such dark grey and patchy stucco that it looked sopping wet. The untidy curtains seemed to have rooms of blank darkness behind them. Shepherd's-purse grew round the mossy doorstep, where a milk bottle dribbling curdled milk had been knocked over.

"Welcome!" said Miss Despenser, throwing open the door upon such a smell of dampness and decay, such a chaotic litter, that Hester stepped aside to take a last full breath before going in.

"You were right. He *is* behaving abominably," Muriel said to Robert as they danced.

Rex had reconnoitred, got his bearings, soon left Lady Bewick's niece, and now was slipping out through the flap of the marquee with a girl in a green frock. Muriel saw his hand pass down the back of his gleaming hair in an anticipatory gesture as he went.

"He's lost no time in finding the most common-looking little minx in the room," she told Robert. She was unsteady and almost breathless with frustration, not getting her own way. So far she had danced once with the doctor and the rest of the time with Robert.

It's his duty, if nothing else, she thought. But Rex and his duty made a casual relationship. Am I so faded that he would rather be rude? But Rex was firstly doing what he wanted to do. If rudeness was involved, it was only as a side issue. It is because he knows I am inaccessible, she told herself.

They continued to catch brief glimpses of Rex during the evening—at the bar, at the buffet. Someone else took Lady Bewick's niece to supper. As it grew later the sky deepened its blue behind the black shapes of the garden trees—the monkey-puzzles darkly barbed, the cedars, and the yews clipped into pagodas and peacocks. Voices floated across the lawns, long skirts brushed the grass. In twos, the dancers strolled in the enclosed warmth of the walled garden, sat on the terrace among the clipped statues, or gazed down at the silvered lily leaves in the pool.

"A good thing we *didn't* bring Hester," Muriel said. "Rex would have left her stranded."

"Sorry!" said Robert as they fell out of step. They had never danced well together, yet they went on dancing. There was nothing to walk in the garden *for*, amongst all that pulsating romance—at their age.

In the end Muriel's dance with Rex was accidental, during a Paul Jones. Hearing the first romping bars of this, she was all for going to the bar, but Lady Bewick hustled her into it—"Now, *everyone!* You must"; and took her by the hand and led her to the circle. They revolved with absurd smiles, feeling looked-over by the encircling men. Robert's expression was one of sudden gaiety, as if he were let off the leash for a moment. How many years has he had that suit? Muriel wondered. Since he was at school, I should think. The sleeves are too short. He looks buttoned-up, spry, like a cock-sparrow. What can a young girl see in him, unless a father? Yet could not that be a danger, especially if Robert were at the same time looking for a daughter? Rex bowed mockingly as he passed her; but his eyes were instantly elsewhere.

An absurd game, like a child's, Muriel thought, feeling outraged and also secretly dismayed at the thought of the music stopping as she faced blankness; then to trail disconsolately to a chair, watched by Robert and by Rex. She had not learned how to mind less than as a little girl at parties—the panic of not being chosen, the first seeds of self-mistrust.

But when the music stopped she was at once in the doctor's arms again. He came straight forward with his arms outstretched; easy to dance with, he waltzed away with her, bouncy, soft-treading, his rounded paunch doing the guiding. By fate or by manoeuvre, Rex had the green girl. Muriel could not see Robert and was inattentive to the dance as she tried to search him out. Then she saw him at the edge of the room. He had been left without a partner and now was going forward to claim a very plain woman in a pink frock and tortoise-shell-rimmed glasses. Muriel was at peace until the next round. It was then that she found herself between Rex and another man when the music stopped. Both hesitated; then Rex seemed to master his unwillingness, smiled, and stepped forward. Authoritatively he took her over, automatically pressed her to him. She made some remark, and, while his eyes still roved round the room, he smiled again and laid his cheek to her hair. "What did you say?"

I am his headmaster's wife! Muriel thought indignantly; but her heart had cantered away.

She *will* be angry, Robert thought as he caught sight of her. But it was she who had suggested bringing him. Robert—blame-evading—had known that Rex would behave like a bounder. Then, to his amazement, he saw that Muriel was smiling. She looked up at Rex, who shook his head teasingly, and then sank deftly back to his nestling embrace.

Rex's eyes stopped following the girl in the green dress, for there was fun closer at hand.

"We shouldn't keep Mrs. Brimmer waiting too long," Miss Despenser said. She put the scrubbing brush down on the hall table. "I must give the cat his supper before we go. Wander about. Make yourself at home."

A great gooseberry-eyed striped cat walked stiffly out of the darkness, stretched, hooped up its back. "Naughty cat, doesn't deserve supper. What is this? Another mess on the Soumak rug?" She took some newspaper from the clutter on the table and bent down to wipe at the clotted fringe. The cat leaned against her legs as she did so, staring up at Hester, callously detached.

"Well, that's that!"

But it wasn't, and to escape the smell Hester followed her to the kitchen, thinking: Only the graves can she keep clean.

In the kitchen the richness of litter was as if a great cornucopia of dirty dishes and decaying food had been unloaded over tables, chairs, shelves, and stove. Flies had stopped their circling and eating and excreting for the day and now slept on the walls and ceiling. Miss Despenser tipped a cod's head out of a saucepan onto a dish on the floor, and Hester half-faintly wished she had stayed in the hall. The cat sniffed at the boiled, clouded eyes and walked away.

"Have you no help?" Hester asked.

"Not now. Gone are the days, alas! when there was a maid to do my hair. But if a woman of my age cannot dress her own hair she should be quite ashamed."

"But not your hair. I meant all the dishes."

"I have all day."

She picked up a sticky-looking wineglass and drank something from it. "That was careless of me," she said. "I hate waste. And now for Mrs. Brimmer!"

How sweet the outside air! Hester thought. As they walked down the lane to the village warmth flowed between the hedges, and she felt a great lassitude and unhappiness.

Miss Despenser struck along beside her, seemed conscious of her mood, and kept glancing up—like some nauseating little dog asking for attention, Hester thought, and looked at the hedgerow, ignoring her.

"If they're not good to you at that school, I am not surprised," Miss Despenser said at last. "I didn't like the wife. And he's as poor a nincompoop as ever there was, I think. Niminy piminy; but *she*'s a thundering dunderhead, as my father used to call the vicar. There was a beautiful panel in the drawing room, and she has moved it away and put shelves up for her collection of mediocre china. It was a clever painting with a great deal of work in it. Detail—rich in detail. Neptune, d'you know, simply smothered in barnacles and seaweed; sea-serpents; tritons; dolphins. A great painstaking monsterpiece. I suppose she thought it indecent. The boys would've liked it, I am sure. If ever things get too much for you, you know, you must come and tuck in with me—at any time of the day or night. I have a spare room—Linda's room."

Hester tried not to imagine poor Miss Linda's room (herself tucking into it), where she had lived, "not quite all there," and probably died.

"They are good to me," she said.

"I thought you seemed rather on the mopy side."

"No."

"Perhaps in love?"

"Not in love. No."

"Linda and I once were—with the same man, fortunately. That was nice. We could discuss him at night. We always shared everything. Oh, we used to laugh, comparing notes, d'you know. If we met him—he used to ride a grey mare called Mirabella (you see, I remember the name, even)—he always raised his hat. Once I was hurrying to the post with a letter in my hand, and he stopped and offered to take it for me." She paused, reflecting on this long-ago kindness, then said, "Well, you *ought* to be in love, I should say. Now is the time for it. Ah, there is Mrs. Brimmer on the lookout for me."

In the lighted bar-window of the pub a huge cardiganed woman appeared. She raised her arms and laid a cloth over a birdcage, then receded. She did not seem to see Miss Despenser.

Over the pub doorway Hester saw the notice: "Melanie Brimmer, licensed to sell Beer, Wines, or Spirits."

"Here I am at last, Mrs. Brimmer," Miss Despenser said, stepping into the flagged passageway.

Mrs. Brimmer, behind the bar, nodded vaguely at them. She then opened a bottle of Guinness, which seemed to flop into the glass in an exhausted way, and beside this she placed a glass of Madeira.

"Will you have the same?" Miss Despenser asked Hester.

"The same as which?"

"I like to sip at both." Miss Despenser began to pull at her skirts and pat herself, and at last brought out a purse.

"Oh, I should like—if I could have a sherry . . ." (Oh, God! I didn't know it would be a pub! she thought. I have no money—nothing.) Again she felt like running.

The sherry was handed to her by the silent Mrs. Brimmer.

"And you yourself, Mrs. Brimmer?"

At last Mrs. Brimmer spoke. "No, I won't touch anything tonight, if it's the same to you. I had one of my turns after tea." She began to tap her fingers rhythmically between her lower ribs. "Heartburn. Stew keeps repeating." She belched softly and gravely.

Hester sipped, then moved her eyes slowly round the room. Two old men played dominoes at a trestle table. By the empty fireplace Hugh Baseden had risen from his chair and stood waiting awkwardly to be recognized.

After the next absurd circling in the dance Muriel faced a blank; the chain of men had thinned, broken, just in front of her as the music stopped. Robert, not far away, knowing how she hated to feel conspicuous or unclaimed even in the smallest ways, made a little gesture of frustration to her, as if to say he would have helped her if he could. She smiled and put on an exaggeratedly woebegone expression and moved aside.

"Time to knock off for the old noggin," Rex said, putting his arm through hers. He had been a fighter-pilot in the war and in certain situations tended to resuscitate the curious mélange of archaisms and slang which once had been his everyday language.

"So you were left too?"

"I didn't go in. I was stooging round the perim as it were, on the lookout."

"Oh, I see."

"I hope you have no objection, ma'am."

"None."

After two whiskies they went into the garden. The music came to an end with a jarring clash of cymbals, then clapping; but Rex and Muriel walked on down the terrace.

"The landed gentry don't do themselves half badly," Rex said, slapping a statue across the buttocks as they passed it. "Hardly a hotbed of bolshevism."

Inside the marquee a man's voice rose above the confusion

of sound, which then gradually sank. "Forty-nine!" was shouted and repeated. After a moment clapping broke out again.

"Oh, that is the raffle," Muriel said.

Couples made their way back across the lawns towards the marquee, but she and Rex walked on.

"Do you want to go and see if you have won a bottle of rich old ruby port or something?" he asked. "Let's sit down here, or will it spoil your dress?"

She did not even glance at the stone seat but sat down at once.

"Are you warm enough?" He rearranged her lace stole round her shoulders. Her diamonds shone in the moonlight, and he put his warm hand to her throat and touched them.

"Heavenly!" he said. "You have some lovely jewels, ma'am."

Perhaps he is going to steal them, she thought in a flash of panic and candour with herself. I must have been deluded to think he just wanted to be with me. But his hand turned over and lay palm down against her beating throat. Or he will strangle me first, she thought, putting nothing past him.

"Why did you ask me to come tonight?" he asked. "You don't like me, do you?"

She closed her eyes.

"Do you?" he persisted. "So often I've seen your face go smooth and expressionless at things I've said."

"I don't understand men like you."

"What sort of man am I, then?"

She had an impulse to flatter him, though it was strange for her to flatter any man. "Although I'm older than you, you make me feel inexperienced and immature."

"It wasn't that," he said. "You were just plainly looking down your nose at me, ma'am."

"Don't call me 'ma'am,' " she whispered.

"What then?"

For a moment she didn't answer and then murmured, "I don't know."

"Mustn't call you 'Muriel.' Not respectful in one so young, so junior. Mrs. Evans, then?"

He slid his hand down her throat and under her armpit. She began to tremble, and at this he leaned forward and kissed her.

"I might call you 'darling,' " he suggested. "I wonder how that would sound."

"This is absurd," she said shakily. "We must go back."

"Back to the marquee, or back to where we were before tonight?"

"Both."

"Just as you say, my dear." He moved away from her, but she did not move. He let the humiliation of this sink into her for a moment, then took her hands. Her fingers twisted restlessly in his, but fastening and not freeing themselves. Nothing so avid as a married woman, he thought complacently and began to kiss her and embrace her in ways of the most extravagant vulgarity, such as she had not encountered outside literature.

In the Hand and Flowers political discussion, though not really raging, was of enough strength to redden cheeks.

There were two periods of acrimony during the evening, Mrs. Brimmer knew. The first was soon after opening time, when the regulars came in fresh from the six-o'clock news and such disasters as it had announced. Later some of the contentious went home to their supper; others stayed and played darts. By eight o'clock a different clientele, more genial, out for the evening, had begun to arrive. Politics at this stage were tabu. Towards closing time, however, geniality might wear thin and argument erupt in one place after another. Mrs. Brimmer, leaning on the bar or going ponderously down into the cellar to bring up the half-slopped pots of beer, was always brief or silent unless describing her indigestion, but towards ten o'clock she would sometimes say abruptly, "I'm Labour, anyway," as in a few minutes she would say, "Time now, gentlemen." Mrs. Brimmer held one or two unexpected opinions which were, all the same, ground inextricably into her personality. Another of her beliefs which she often made clear was that women should not go into public houses. She served them silently and grudgingly, and would have horsewhipped every one, she often said. She really did not approve of drinking at all, apart from the gin-and-pep she sometimes took to shift her wind. However, having lived in the pub as a wife, she duly carried on as a widow.

"What they want is to have us all equal," Miss Despenser said, "and the only way to do that is to level everyone *down*—not to raise everyone *up*. No, it's down, down, down, all the time. When we're finally in the gutter, then we shall have true democracy."

"But surely—" said Hugh Baseden.

"When I was young everyone was better off, and do you know why?"

"Well—"

"Because we all knew our proper places. No one was

ashamed to serve. Why, my mother's maid was like a sister to her. Two sisters. Peas in a pod."

"That's right." Mrs. Brimmer nodded.

"But when she had helped your mother to dress she didn't go to the dance with her. She stayed and tidied the bedroom," Hester said. She glanced at Hugh, who looked gravely back in agreement. Some of his gravity, however, was his anxiety at Hester's having drunk too much.

"She didn't want to go. That is what I am saying. She didn't want to go. That is why she was so happy."

"My mother was in service," one of the dominoes players said. "Happiest days of her life, she reckoned. No worries. All found."

"There you are, you see," Miss Despenser said.

"It's wrong to be happy like that—not to have your own life," Hester said. At the back of her mind she felt a great sense of injustice somewhere, of sacrifices which ought not to be asked or made. "Kowtowing," she murmured and, looking flushed and furious, sipped her sherry.

"Kowtowing fiddlededee," Miss Despenser said. "You talk as if the educated classes exist for nothing."

Mrs. Brimmer drew her blouse away from her creased chest, glanced down mysteriously, blowing gently between her breasts, then fanned herself. "I hear Charlie's gone," she said.

"He's gone, has he?" asked the gaitered gamekeeper. His setters stretched by the fire, blinking their bloody eyes, nosing their private parts.

"So Les Salter said when he came with his club money."

"I said to the missus, 'I reckon old Charlie's going at

last.' I said that only last night when I saw the lamp upstairs."

"That's right."

"When was that?"

"This morning. They sent along for Mrs. Brown about eight o'clock. He'd just gone then."

"Would you like a drink?" Hugh asked Miss Despenser.

"Most kind."

"What may I get you?"

"Mrs. Brimmer knows."

He stood awkwardly before Hester. "The same?" If I take her back drunk, I take the blame too, I suppose, he thought. To his relief she shook her head.

"How are you getting home?" he asked quietly.

"I shall look after her," Miss Despenser said, and she laid her hand on Hester's arm. Hester looked down at it with loathing. Under the shiny, loose skin the high veins seemed to writhe and knot themselves as if separately alive.

Nothing was said. Hugh turned to the bar and watched Mrs. Brimmer reluctantly pouring out the drinks.

"He is rather familiar," Miss Despenser said. "After all, he is not quite in the same position as you. You could spend the night with me if you are nervous."

To be saved for one night from her dreams would be so very wonderful, she thought. She and Hester could sit up until morning and talk. Her dreams were usually distressing. There was one in which her father kept entering the library, always from the same door, crossing the room, disappearing, only to come in again in the same way, with the dread inevitability of dreams. Then there was the one in which her mother told her to pull down her clothes, but her skirts shrank and shrank. Because of her nightmares she had tried to sleep in the daytime, for bad dreams come in the dark; but to be awake in the quiet house—especially as it seemed to be only *just* quiet—was frightening too.

"I will pop a hot bottle in your bed," she promised. "You are not to think it will be a trouble."

"I must go home. There is no reason why I should not."

Miss Despenser bent her head. "I daresay you think me very frumpish," she said. "Can't be helped. We all come to it. Most kind," she said again to Hugh, but gave Mrs. Brimmer a sharp glance as a Guinness only was placed before her. Mrs. Brimmer was once more glancing nonchalantly inside her blouse.

"Is she cooking something down there?" Hugh muttered as he sat down beside Hester, and then in an even lower voice asked, "May I walk home with you?"

"But how can I get rid of her?" Hester asked, and felt soiled by her disloyalty.

"Time, gentlemen, if you please." Mrs. Brimmer went to the door and opened it, letting in cool air and moths.

"I will see you home," Miss Despenser told Hester. "But let *him* get on his way first." She slowly drained her Guinness, keeping her eyes shut. When she opened them Hugh Baseden was still there. "Good night!" she bade him. Froth was drying on her moustached upper lip, and Hugh looked away from her as he spoke. "I am taking Hester back to the school. May we see you home first?"

"Good *night!*" said Mrs. Brimmer, not caring who went with whom, as long as all went without delay.

They set off together and Miss Despenser was sullen, and

her course vague and veering. Once she stumbled against the high bank and, hoping to steady herself, put her hand down into a patch of nettles. She righted herself and wandered on, rubbing her inflamed wrist, drawing herself obstinately away from Hugh when he tried to support her. But when they reached her house she allowed him to take her key and open the door. He switched on the light, and she sat down abruptly on a chair in the hall. When Hester said good night she just nodded without lifting her head to see her go, and stared at the cat, who seemed to have waited for her to come home before he squatted in a corner and began to wet the carpet. She did not rebuke him, but sat still for a long time, and at last tears began to slant out of her eyes and down the sides of her face. Not since Linda died! she thought. For Hester, that stranger to her, had come up out of a mist or a dream to confront her with loneliness. Unsteadily she stood up and crossed the hall. The looking-glass was filmed with damp and dust, but she could see herself dimly in it. Clutching the back of a chair, she rocked to and fro, staring. "It is what I am," she told herself. "It is what I live with." Her vision seemed to slide and slip like colours in a kaleidoscope. "Pussy!" she called. "Naughty pussy! Now where are you?" He came swaying out of the kitchen, paw before paw, coat rippling, pupils only dark slits, tail curved. I am master here, he seemed to say.

"Who was that tipsy, titupping little person?" Hugh Baseden asked.

"I met her once when I was wandering around. She is mad, I think."

"The stench in that house! Is she a witch?"

"I expect so."

"I didn't know what to think when you walked in with her."

"I have to go somewhere."

"Do—*they* know?"

"Neither know nor care."

They climbed the bank and began to cross the field, towards the wood.

"You must be very lonely," he said. "I have often thought that. I suppose they're very nice, though so terribly set in their complacent ways. And when they do do something enjoyable—this dance, I mean—they leave you at home."

"I didn't want to go—like Miss Despenser's mother's maid."

"And Robert's a kind chap, but such a very dry old stick. Very fussy to work for."

"Very fussy." Hester panted, breathless from the steep field path.

"Of course he's your uncle. I shouldn't have said that."

"My cousin—my cousin."

"He has some rather old-maidish ways, you know—peering over his glasses, taking pills."

"And the barometer!" Hester was astonished to hear herself saying. "Tapping it at least three times a day. Why not just take the weather as it comes?"

They entered the warm wood, and this time she was not afraid.

"*She* is the dominant one, of course," Hugh said.

Hester thought: Perhaps I was only scared not to be in love with someone—anybody. She was confused by her sudden sensations of irritability towards Robert. "My head!"

she said and stumbled along over the tree roots, pressing both hands to her temples.

"I will find you some of Rex's famous hangover pills when we get back. It was funny about Rex going tonight."

"Funny?"

"I thought madam's view of him was very dark indeed." He took Hester's elbow and guided her out of the way of some low branches. "Nearly there," he said.

The air was thinner and cooler outside the wood. They came to the churchyard and the neat Despenser graves.

Muriel had creamed her face and was weeping. Robert was silent with frightening displeasure.

"I don't want to see him again," she cried.

He took the cuff-links out of his shirt and put them back into their velvet-padded box. He said, "That is what you cannot help doing. It is a little awkwardness you have created for us all."

"He might resign."

"But he won't, and there is no reason why he should. You will find he is quite unperturbed. It will have meant nothing to him," Robert added cruelly. "When he remembers, and if it amuses him, he may take advantage of the situation to discomfit us. It is dreadfully late to be crying so," he said fretfully. "I am so tired, and he will see your red eyes in the morning and purr more than ever."

"Robert, you are rather working this up. By the way you are speaking I might have committed adultery."

"I think you might if you hadn't suddenly heard 'God Save the Queen.' Your patriotism made you stand up—even if it *was* in each other's arms."

"Oh, the brittle wit! How dare you? We had suddenly realized that the dance was over."

"Time had stood still."

She began angrily to splash cold water on her eyes. When she was in bed she said shakily, "After all, *you* don't make love to me."

He got neatly into bed and lay down as far from her as he could, his back turned.

"Do you?" She wept.

"You know I do not, and you know why I do not."

"If I didn't like it, perhaps that was your fault. Did you ever think of that?"

"Very often. I surveyed every explanation in turn. Then I became rather bored and thought: So be it."

"I know I was wrong tonight—though really sillier than wrong."

"You made us both look absurd and started a ridiculous scandal by your behaviour. Everyone missed you. I suppose it was an arranged thing between you. I remember your insistence on having him there. How long, if you wouldn't mind telling me, has this romance been flourishing?" He spoke stiffly, lying with his back to her. He was anxious to be reassured, to shake off the insecurity which results from a serious deviation in one we have trusted.

"You shall not say such a thing," she cried.

He had gone too far in his suspicions, and her amazed rejection of them was so genuine that he now went too far in his relief, although he only gravely said, "I apologize."

This dreadful conversation, he thought. The cold phrases of hatred—"I apologize," "How dare you!" "You *know* why."

"If it was just a sudden, ill-judged thing," he said, "I can understand better. Anything else—plotting, lying—would not have been like you."

She lay on her back and stared up through the darkness, said, "Thank you," in a far-away voice.

"Oh, don't cry again." He turned over and touched her hair.

"We were so happy," she cried.

"I don't think we were very happy."

"I was."

He meant his silence to punish her. To explain—she thought—everything, to simplify everything and press the punishment back upon him, she said, "If Hester had never come here! If we could be as we were!"

"She had no part in this. She was utterly innocent."

"Her innocence has been like a poison to us. It has corrupted us both." In her mind she seemed to step back from the thought of their married life, as if she recoiled physically from an unexpected horror. She said, "It is like the time when I found the adders lying under the ferns."

"What is like that?" he asked. His head lay on his crooked arm, and he stared into the darkness, where there was less to see than behind his closed lids.

"To realize my ignorance about you; to discover our estrangement—this tangle of secrets; and to know that I can behave as I did tonight."

"Don't cry, Muriel."

"Why do you call me 'Muriel'? You have never done so until now, until lately." Until Hester came, both thought.

"She—Hester, I mean—has made no difference to us. I'm not in love with her, if that is any comfort—if you want to hear such embarrassing things really said aloud." He spoke coldly and angrily and with a sense of treachery to himself, as if she had forced from him some alien oath. "She has changed nothing—only shown us what existed, exists."

"We should be very grateful for that." Her burst of anger was a relief from tears.

If I can never love her again, he thought, why is it Hester's fault? It is she, Muriel, who destroyed it, let it slip from her, and then, in trying to have it back again, broke it forever. Lying so close to her, he let this monstrous treason against her form in the darkness. Then he felt her lift herself up on one elbow. She was wiping her eyes. Crying was over, then? But, more dread to him even than her weeping, she put out her hand and touched his arm, and he wondered if she had sensed the fissure widening, separating her from him, in his heart—the hard knowledge of non-love. She began to throw words into this abyss as if to close it before too late. "Robert, forgive me! I will try. I will do everything. I am sorry. I cannot bear it."

The words worked no magic and continued into unseemliness, he thought. His reserve had changed to coldheartedness, and he wondered how he could ever change it back again. He turned over and put his arms round her.

"Let us try again!" she begged, and she pressed her burning eyes against his shoulder. He moved his head back a little, for her hair had fallen against his mouth.

"We will both try!" he whispered. "I will try very hard." But will it be any use? he wondered.

Robert, in days that followed, wondered if it were the mildness of his nature that enabled him to find the suppression of love more easy than the suppression of non-love. No concentration could cure him of his lack of feeling towards Muriel, and, to ward off his indifference to her he began, without knowing it, to catalogue her virtues. In this way he always had a ready antidote for the irritations she caused him, and quickly smothered thoughts of her coldness with remembrances of her kindness to animals and that servants loved her. Against her sarcasm he recalled her loyalty, and tried to acknowledge her steadfastness when beset by her lack of humour.

At first, as if a true understanding were between them, Muriel went through her days in chastened peace of mind, submissive and forgiving. Emotion had tired her and she seemed weakly convalescent, her mind on such little things, as if she only waited for the time to pass. At night the resentment she fought during the day poisoned her dreams, so that, lying beside Robert with her heart full of love for him, she dreaded to fall asleep and so out of love again—would wake trembling or tearful at his dream-betrayals, carrying imaginary wrongs beyond the dawn, to discolour all the morning.

Bravely she set out to enchant him all over again as she had done so many years ago, but disheartened now, frightened, and lacking the equipment of romanticism, energy, curiosity. For I did not have him once for all, she thought sadly, arranging her pink dress against the red carpet and her white hands on the tapestry; glancing timidly at him, who did not look in her direction. Her voice lost its edge when she spoke to him, but only Hester noticed the new warmth, and was embarrassed.

"It will soon be Speech Day," Muriel said. "Will last

year's hat do, Robert? Or would that look as if the school were going downhill?"

"I should buy a new one—for your sake, not the school's. I can't imagine parents remembering a hat from one year to the next."

"Hester and I can't agree with that."

Hester did not raise her eyes.

For the first time Muriel was self-conscious at Speech Day, watched the great marquee going up, arranged flowers, and finally pinned on her new cartwheel hat, feeling unusual sensations of flurried dread. "Exquisite!" Rex whispered, passing her as she crossed the hall. Until that moment the evening of the dance, for him, might never have been. He was as heedless as a bird snatching at berries along a hedgerow.

Muriel stood beside Robert and shook hands with the parents and felt that beneath their admiration these people did not like her; fathers were overawed and mothers were doubtful—unsure as to whether she really loved their sons as they deserved. Hester watched her; Rex watched her; Robert looked away from her; tiredness overtook her.

In the evening she telephoned Beatrice—her only friend, she now felt; though more than a friend: perhaps an extension of her own personality and her own experiences (sometimes sullying) greedily grafted onto the weaker parts of Beatrice's nature. Oh, God, let her not be out! she prayed, imagining the telephone ringing and ringing in the empty house. But Beatrice, breathless from hurrying, soon answered and lost her mystery in doing so, became accessible, too easily summoned.

"I was in the garden. How did it go, darling? I thought of you. Was the hat right? Did Robert love it?"

"He didn't say he didn't."

"And tea and everything? And Robert's speech?"

"Yes. Beatrice, if I call in will you come for a drive before dinner? My head aches. The last ones have only just gone away."

"Oh, parents!" she said later. They drove along the lanes, down the hill past the Hand and Flowers, where Mrs. Brimmer stood at the doorway in the sun. "Perhaps I just hate them because they have children," Muriel said.

The car was open and the soft air flowed over them, lifting their hair, but none of the peace of the evening reached Muriel, who drove fast, noticed nothing, frowned at the road ahead. "You've had children, Beatrice, and you cannot *know* . . ."

"Darling, you are overtired."

"No. For years it has been so improbable that I should ever have a child that I stopped thinking about it. I might have been shocked, perhaps, to find myself pregnant. But now, just lately, knowing for sure that I never could be, that in *this* lifetime, and for *this* woman, it couldn't ever happen, I feel panicky, want to go back, be different, have another chance. I can't explain." She changed gears badly, was driving carelessly.

"Do slow down," Beatrice said.

"I'm sorry."

"I never think about having children now," Beatrice said. "All the business bores me enormously, like some hobby one has discarded. When I hear of younger women having them I even feel slightly surprised, for it all seems too finished with and démodé. They think they are being so clever and can't know how I lack interest. I just think, Goodness me, are people still doing *that*?"

"But you'll have grandchildren and then you'll be caught up in it again."

"I suppose so." She looked smug.

"Where are we going?" Muriel asked. "I *ought* to be going home."

She drove on, brushing the cow-parsley in the ditch, swerving as a bird flew up suddenly from some horse-droppings on the road.

"Very sorry! Then the holidays will soon come," she said, as if continuing the same plaint. "The three of us left alone together."

"Has nothing been done about her going?"

"There is nowhere for her to go."

"You should go away yourself. I would come with you if you liked. You need a holiday."

"And leave them together?"

"Oh, no, of course."

They laughed shakily. Muriel said, "It is as well one still has a sense of humour."

"Thank you, Hester, for all your help," Robert said. He handed her a drink and, taking up his own, asked if she had seen Muriel.

"No." She had watched her driving away, but thought that Muriel could explain her own comings and goings.

"And I heard her asking Hugh in for a drink. You look

very smart, Hester." But it was too robustly said, not tender. "I suppose it all went off all right. At any rate, it went off. Muriel is splendid at that sort of thing. Never complains, as most women would, although I can see it all seems a great deal of nonsense to her."

Before Hugh came Robert was called away to the telephone, and Hester was left alone. The day had tired and confused her, for she had never been quite sure of her duties. Ashamed to stand idle, she had tried to attach herself to the other workers, but Matron's campaign of defence had not included her. She had managed to hand a few cups of tea and annoyed the senior boys by doing so. Few things are so fatiguing as standing by to help and not being called upon, and now her feet, her back, even her teeth, were aching. She drank her sherry and put the glass on the chimney-piece. Wavering clumsily, her hand touched a china figure and knocked it into the hearth. She gave a quick glance at the door, then stooped down to see what damage was done. Muriel's favourite Dresden girl lay in the fender; an arm carrying a gilt basket of strawberries was broken off at the elbow. Hester prayed for time, as if that could make the figure whole again; but in a school there are so many footsteps, and any she could hear above the beating blood in her head might be Robert's or Muriel's coming to this room. She pushed the figure behind a bowl of flowers and put the broken piece in her pocket. If she were ever granted a few undisturbed moments she was sure she could have mended it; but now, although no one came and the waiting was unbearable, she could not be certain of being alone. She tried to find a nonchalant pose, sitting on the window seat, far from the fireplace; then saw her sherry glass still there, incriminatingly near to and drawing attention to the empty place. She went to fetch it and on her way back to the window seat thought of refilling it, to give a more natural look to her pose. As she was lifting the decanter, Hugh came in.

Her trembling guilt, the sherry slopped over the table, worried him. They are turning her into a secret drinker, he thought, but her confusion touched him immeasurably, for he knew similar sensations and had learned new refinements of them at Muriel's hands. We are always mopping up for this girl, he thought as he dabbed at the table with his handkerchief. Her misery had gone so far beyond accountable bounds that he began to wonder how much she had drunk.

"Where is everyone?" he asked. He passed his handkerchief under the bottom of the glass before he gave it to her.

"Robert is telephoning."

"And—madame?" For Muriel set up such awkwardnesses in people that they could sometimes not even give her her proper name.

"Went out in the car."

"Who went out in the car?" Robert asked as he came from the hall.

In Hester's shattered face her lips moved stiffly as if from some rigor and at last formed the name.

"Oh, I wondered where she was. She'll be back. Sherry, Hugh?" Robert's bustling about could not conceal his perplexity. If people are liars, who makes them be? he was wondering. "Everything went off well, Hugh?" His voice wavered upwards. "Nothing untoward? No one insulted Matron? Mrs. Vallance seemed incensed at something."

"The wretched boy's cricket boot. She kept saying she would much rather both were lost than only one."

"People often say that, particularly about gloves," Muriel said, hurrying into the room. She went to the mirror and smoothed her hair. "Sorry, Robert! Sorry, Hugh! Oh, and Hester too! I didn't see you hiding in the window seat. I went for a little drive with Beatrice. May I have a drink, darling? And, Hugh, your glass is empty. God, what a day! Never mind, another year until the next one. Darling, Hugh's glass! Dinner is cold and can wait for us for once. I went into the Science Room, Hugh, just to see if you had been up to anything sinister, and I was charmed. The heavenly demonstration of cross-pollination. I do think you are to be congratulated."

Hugh gazed intently into his glass as Robert filled it. He looked as if he were parched with thirst, but sherry was a long way from his thoughts. He knew he was being ridiculed but could not sort it out sufficiently to make an answer. Meaningless innuendo, he decided. And the very worst kind, too, because it finishes the game.

"I did botany at school," Muriel said. "That was considered ladylike even in those days—*particularly* in those days, when we drew no conclusions from it. Purple loosestrife seemed to have nothing in common with us."

"Muriel!" Robert protested. "Your Victorian girlhood doesn't convince us, you know."

She went close to the mirrored over-mantel, leaned forward to her reflection, and once more smoothed her hair. Hester watched in terror the long white hands moving then from hair to flowers, tidying them too. Then the room froze. Muriel picked up the Dresden figure, seemed surprised by genuine grief, paused; then turned to face them, looking dazed and puzzled.

"What a beautiful—thing!" Hugh said, stepping forward, as if she were only asking him to admire it. "The dress is just like real lace."

"Robert!" Muriel cried, ignoring Hugh. Her grief is out of all proportion, Hester thought, remembering the same stunned look of wives in old newsreels, waiting at pit-heads as the stretchers were carried away, or of mothers lifting their babies across the rubble of bombed streets.

Robert asked sharply—as if he foresaw hell for all of them—"How did that happen?" He took the china figure and examined it. Muriel turned back and began to search the chimneypiece.

"Is it broken?" Hugh asked, but no one answered. He was accustomed to that. Hester began to tremble, and clutched the fragment in her pocket as though she might be searched.

"It must be there," Robert said. "One of the maids must have done it without knowing, or they would have told you."

Hester falsely went over and looked into the flower bowl.

"Not there?" Muriel asked.

"No."

"Quite a clean break," Robert said. "It could be mended easily."

"If we find the other piece," said Muriel.

"What is it we are looking for?" Hugh asked.

"I shall have to question the maids," Muriel said. "It has been hidden purposely. They have never deceived me before." She was proud of her relationship with the domestic staff, to whom she was always generous and considerate:

they saw a side of her which was hidden from most people, and they were loyal to her. She delayed the task of questioning them, refilled her glass with sherry, and, as she drank it, went on searching, lifting cushions and rugs and thrusting her fingers down the sides of stuffed chairs until the backs of her hands looked bruised.

Hugh did not dine with them, and Muriel said nothing during the meal. When dishes were brought in she helped herself and ate without raising her eyes, feeling awkwardness with the maid and guilt at her own suspicions.

After dinner Hester went out into the garden and walked in an opposite direction from the church—down an azalea walk to a ferny grotto. The dark, dusty leaves parted and disclosed a little Gothic summerhouse, which was locked so that the boys should not damage it. No one came there—the dark rockiness of the place was chilling, the clay paths slippery in wet weather; the creaking trees were clotted with rooks' nests, and the rooks themselves filled the air with commotion, restlessly calling, circling, dropping again and again to the branches.

Robert had brought her here on her first day, when he had shown her round; he had taken a key from his pocket and unlocked the door for her. The cave-smell was unpleasant to breathe, but she had marvelled aloud at the interior. The walls and domed roof were encrusted with shells in fan patterns set in cement. Light from the coloured glass in the windows shone in patches.

Now she could only stand on tiptoe at the door and look through the wire-covered glass panel. The piece of china from her pocket she forced through the wire and broken pane. It struck the stone floor inside.

"Were you trying to get in?" Hugh asked her, shouting rather above the noise of the rooks.

"No, it is always locked."

"Did I surprise you? I saw you come this way when I was down at the nets with some of the boys. I meant to ask you before dinner if you'd come for a walk, but there was all that rumpus about the ornament—put it out of my mind; I mean, I hadn't a chance. Of course, she has some nice things—madame, Muriel, that is—and she thinks a lot of them. Naturally."

"They were her mother's."

"Nice diamonds, too, Rex was saying."

"Yes."

Hugh began to perceive that Hester lacked interest in Muriel's possessions.

"Never having had anything very valuable myself," he said, "it is hard for me to understand anyone being as upset as she was tonight."

"It is because she hasn't anything valuable," Hester said. "And she knows it."

"Children, you mean?"

"Partly."

They walked down the winding path. Two boys were kneeling by some flint steps, looking for lizards under the stones. Hugh had a little patronizing chat with them, then he and Hester walked on again. The boys exchanged slow winks.

"Did you ever see that horrible old baggage again?" Hugh asked. "The one with the cat."

"No. Not again."

"Are you happy here?"

"Not very."

This was so promising that he made no answer until they reached the seat in the laurel walk where Muriel and Beatrice had sat and talked; then, when he was sitting at Hester's side, he asked, "Why aren't you happy?" Looking round carefully, he made sure there were no boys about, and took her hand.

"I am in the way, you see," Hester said gravely. "I ought not to be here."

When he took her other hand and drew nearer to her, she seemed not to notice. Although her indifference was in a sense discouraging to him, it allowed him to proceed without hindrance. He kissed her, but, still looking rather mopishly before her, she said, "I didn't want to harm anyone. Not even someone I hate."

"You couldn't harm anyone," he said. "You are so entirely gentle."

Some boys shouted in the distance, and he moved promptly aside, learned forward, his elbows on his knees, in an attitude of serious but impersonal discussion. But the voices faded and no one came. A bell rang and he muttered, "Thank God for that," and turned again to Hester and took her in his arms.

In the morning Muriel questioned the maids, Lucy and Sylvia. One showed transparent surprise and concern, the other haughty offendedness; and since each reacted in her own way, as her innocence dictated, Muriel said no more. She often boasted that she knew at once when people were lying, not realizing how little this endeared her to anyone, least of all to Hester, who, never very honest in the easiest of times, was lately finding it almost impossible to tell the truth.

One thing Hester was determined on, and it was to avoid being left alone with Muriel. She managed this all morning and was about to manage it after lunch as she followed Robert to his study, when Muriel, after letting her reach the door, said, "Oh, Hester! If you wouldn't mind—I won't keep you a moment."

Robert walked on as if he had not heard; but by the time he reached his study his agitation was so great, he was so sure of what Muriel would inflict on the girl, that he went out into the hall again and stood guiltily at the table, pretending to read *The Times.*

The voices on the other side of the door were separated by long silences; the blurred murmurings seemed without consequence or meaning. Then he heard Hester crying. The sobs came in a rush towards the door, and in a panic he hurried back to his study and sat down at his desk. He heard footsteps in the hall, and was so sure that they were coming to him and felt so anxious to be ready to deal with disaster—fidgeting busily with papers, continually clearing his throat—that he did not listen, and when at last he realized that the house was silent he could not tell in which direction Hester had gone.

At three o'clock he gave a Latin lesson. Afterwards he returned to his study. She was not there, and the typewriter was still covered. He put down his books and went to look for Muriel; but Muriel, he was told, had gone to a meeting in the village. He spent an idle, worried afternoon, and Hester did not appear. Another man, he thought, could get away from this, could leave the women and go to work! He was forced to remain, always morbidly aware of the atmosphere in the house.

Muriel returned in the early evening, said, "Hello, Robert!" very casually as she took her afternoon's post from the hall table, and walked into the drawing room.

"Where is Hester?"

She read her letters attentively. "I can't tell you. I went out soon after lunch."

"Not soon enough."

She had to raise her head then.

"What have you done to her? You made her cry."

"From no sense of shame, either, I'm afraid. Only from chagrin at being found out."

"I suppose she *did* break that damned thing."

"Exactly."

"She was afraid to tell you. You shouldn't frighten her so."

"She stood there and listened to me saying that I should question Lucy and Sylvia."

"Did you know then that she had done it?"

"I wasn't sure, although she is so clumsy that one's thoughts naturally fly to her."

"You make her clumsy, you know."

"Yes, I daresay it is my fault."

"I know she doesn't always speak the truth, and I worry sometimes that she should be driven to deceit."

"Driven? You choose melodramatic words, Robert. And I can't imagine anyone driving anyone into such fantastic lunatic deceptions as your Hester's."

"You must have upset her very much."

"Yes, as you say, I made her cry. I am glad I did not make Lucy cry. I am glad I took their word at once."

"But where is Hester now?"

Muriel put aside her letters with a sigh of weariness. "I do not know, Robert. I do not know. You have seen her since I."

"But I haven't. I left her here with you."

"The last I saw of her, she was coming to you for the key."

"What key?"

"The key to the Shell House. Where she had hidden the piece of china. I sent her to fetch it and to get the key from you."

"That was her punishment, was it? To have to face me, as she was, and make that pathetic little confession, then go out, humiliated, to pick up the bits? And you can do that to someone just because they have broken some china."

"She has broken more than china for me."

"The deepest destruction is done with finesse, not clumsiness. She couldn't hold a candle to you. I must go to look for her."

He will find her weeping in her room and console her, take sides against me, Muriel thought. She said, "I am at the end of this marriage, Robert. I cannot bear any more of it."

"I will ask Hugh," he said. "Perhaps he will have seen her."

"Why Hugh?"

"Because I think he is in love with her."

"Is that so? I wouldn't have thought it of him. You need not speak so angrily. Poor young man, I don't suppose he has any idea of how he is trespassing. Anyone else would know, but he's a little extra-stupid." Once again she desired to strike him, did so with words instead. "I expect she is just sulking in her bedroom, so I shouldn't fuss."

But Hester was not in her room, and those who were discreetly questioned had not seen her.

Fortune struck blindingly at Miss Despenser. All fell into place and she saw that, given the right ingredients and patience, heart's desire at last will come, like risen bread, to proving point. She had despaired in loneliness, then conquered her despair, up to that stage of no-feeling where the mind goes joggety-jog on little errands of the will, each minute measured out in a tiny sip. For time heals all, she told herself. At the end of life we should be quite healed, and so go whole to dissolution.

Mrs. Brimmer, towards two o'clock, had mysteriously run out of both Guinness and Madeira; could only suggest a mild-and-bitter, and then the bitter had given out. The men sniggered. "You know I don't like cold drinks," Miss Despenser complained. "You should write to the brewers!"

"I will," Mrs. Brimmer said, and they laughed again.

Mother would be shocked, Miss Despenser thought as she wandered home. The way they speak nowadays.

It seemed siesta time in the lanes. Only the bees moved. But the house was buzzing with activity. Green and dark blue flies were delirious over the plates of cat's food in the kitchen. In sudden disgust with her life, Miss Despenser took them all up and threw them—dishes too—into the dustbin, and started a furious zigzagging as she lifted the lid.

At that moment Hester rang the bell.

"What luck!" said Miss Despenser when she opened the door. "You came just at the right time. I was doing a bit of spring cleaning, and I shall be glad to knock off and have a chat. You will cheer me up, I know you."

Hester, trembling, swollen-eyed, entered the house. She bore her nausea for the sake of Muriel's punishment, knowing she could not hope to hurt her without sacrificing herself—had even contemplated, in a brief moment of rage, the supreme sacrifice, for no greater hatred could she show than that.

"I knew it would be a red-letter day," Miss Despenser said and handed Hester a postcard, "when this came this morning. I don't often have anything in the post," she explained simply.

It was a printed invitation from a girls' school. *Tennis Match,* Hester read. *Past v. Present. 2:15 sharp.* "What is Asboga?" she asked dully and pressed her fingers to her burning eyes.

"Abbey School, Brighton, Old Girls' Association," Miss Despenser said. "Linda and I were both Asbogs. Though she could only stand a term there. It was the happiest time I ever had, although at times we pined for each other. The food was so good. I don't think you could better that food anywhere. On Fridays we had a red jelly with bananas sliced up in it. Every Friday. We looked forward to it, I can tell you. What is the food like where you are? What did you have for luncheon today, for instance?"

Hester thought, then said, "A sort of shepherd's pie."

"My favourite! And after?"

"Oh, dear, I don't know."

"But it can only have been half an hour ago."

"I think it was apple—something with apple . . ." She began to cry again.

"Now, chin up! Surely you don't grizzle over your food like poor Linda? She once cried over an apple charlotte. She cried all afternoon without stopping. My father made her sit there till teatime. She ate it in the end. He had a will of iron. I advise you to eat up in the beginning."

"I don't want to answer questions, that's all," Hester said.

"You look peaky. Come along, hop onto the sofa, legs up! I'll make you a cup of tea."

Hester lay down, the dusty plush against her cheek. Misery obliterated her. Someone take over, take charge, take care! She wept for a little while, then fell asleep.

Miss Despenser was a long time getting the tea ready. She worked happily but slowly, in her usual state of afternoon muzziness.

After dinner Robert found Hugh walking about the grounds and asked if he had seen Hester.

"No, I was looking for her."

"She didn't come to dinner, and I am rather anxious."

"Has there been some upset?" Hugh asked at once.

"Yes. Why do you ask?"

"She seemed fairly miserable last night. We went for a walk, you know. Is she in her room?"

"No. Of course we looked there first. I'll stroll about and keep my eyes open."

When he had shaken off Hugh, Robert went quickly up the path to the Shell House and unlocked the door. It swung open with a grating sound. The piece of china lay on the dusty floor, proving nothing but what Muriel had said, that Hester had delivered herself into her hands.

He began an aimless search of the grounds, for he could

not think where Hester might go, or what she did in her spare time. Some of the boys watched him with excitement, for they were sure he was out on some mysterious investigation, and they wondered if school monotony might be enlivened after prayers next day by the announcement of some appalling scandal—some of the lordly ones found smoking in the shrubbery, or the copy of *Lady Chatterley's Lover* unearthed. When he was seen to be walking more quickly towards the churchyard, as if struck by a sudden idea, he was watched intently by one boy, Terence Mooney, who always made his beer in the little shed by the church. His father was a brewer—Mooney's Sunshine Ales—and Terry's school life was an everlasting misery in consequence. "You must know how to make it," the boys said. "Surely your old man told you. Well, write and ask him, then."

He had pretended to write to ask, and the boys gathered round and watched him open his next letter from home—"Darling, I hope you are happy and your earache better. Don't talk after lights out, but get all the rest you can. . . ."

"Did he say anything?"

"Yes, of course."

"Well, what?"

"Well, he says I mustn't say. It's a family secret."

"Well, you're his family, aren't you? Can't he tell you?"

"Yes."

"Well, get on, then. We don't want to know how you do it. We just want to drink it."

"It takes time. It has to ferment, you see."

"All right, we'll give you time." They arranged to give him a week. He studied encyclopædias. He did not sleep. He stole potatoes and brewed concoctions. These never tasted right to him, or to most of the boys, who made it clear that they would never touch Mooney's beer when they left school and could choose. Terry lived in wretched unpopularity, busy, furtive; he segregated his parents on Speech Day, and now, watching Robert, wondered if he would be expelled.

"Mr. Baseden's prowling about too," a boy said. "He went though the churchyard a few minutes ago."

"They might be going for walks," poor Mooney said.

"Not them. They keep looking round."

It did not occur to them that masters could have anything but boys in their minds.

Hugh went to the Hand and Flowers, but neither Miss Despenser nor Hester was there. "I'm not breaking my heart, either," Mrs. Brimmer said as she drew his beer. He drank it quickly and hurried back up the lane to the stucco villa.

"No, there's no one there," Miss Despenser told Hester, who had heard the knocking on the door. "I often fancy the same thing; but nobody calls here. Perhaps Pussy jumped down off my bed. It wouldn't be anyone."

But at the second knock Hester went to the window. Hugh, stepping back from the porch, saw her behind the dusty pane. She had a fan of old photographs in her hand and her face was stained with tears.

"Yes. It is Hugh Baseden," she said, and he could see her lips moving as she still stared at him.

"Then draw the curtains. How dare he trespass here! Peering and prying!"

Hester, dreamy with weakness, moved towards the hall and opened the door. She was at a stage of recovery from grief—the air was vacant, silence enfolded her, and when she put out her hand to the wall to steady herself after the effort of opening the door, the wall seemed to bend, to slope away from her; and it was as if Hugh's hand as she touched it dissolved, vanished.

He lifted her and carried her to a chair in the hall. "Put your head down," he told her. She obeyed. Her hand with the photographs swung against the floor. Pussy came up and walked in a figure of eight round her feet. Hugh pushed him aside.

"And now, Paul Pry, you can leave my house at once," Miss Despenser said. "I was just coming into the hall when I saw what you did to Pussy. You peer through my windows, force your way in, are cruel to my cat, and goodness knows what you have done to this poor girl. Sit up, Hester! The blood will run to your head."

Hester sat up, and Hugh pushed her head down again.

"You blockhead!" Miss Despenser shouted. "She will faint, you great dunce, if you are not careful."

He knelt down before Hester and held her head against him.

"She was all right until you came," Miss Despenser said. "I wish you would go away again."

"What are these?" Hugh asked, gently taking the photographs from Hester.

"They are mine. I am showing them to her," Miss Despenser said. "We haven't nearly finished yet." She sprang forward and snatched up one of the photographs he had dropped. "How dare you throw my things on the floor, you blundering oaf! That is my sister." She looked, with a change to tenderness, at the yellowed card, the girl with the vapid smile, the hand resting on a carved pedestal behind which a backcloth of roses and pillars met the carpet unevenly.

"Are you well enough to come home?" Hugh asked Hester. "Shall I get a car?"

"I can't go home."

"No, she can't go home."

"What is wrong?" Hugh asked softly, kneeling by her, rocking her gently in his arms.

"It is out of the question," Miss Despenser said. "Now you must run along. I am sorry I cannot invite you to dinner." She fought bravely, but by now she knew that she was going to lose. He had forgotten her as an adversary, while he listened to Hester's story.

"Get up off your knees!" Miss Despenser tried to interrupt them. "You exhibitionist!"

"I don't know why I did," Hester was moaning. "I lost my nerve. She makes me behave badly. I hate her. Oh, I hate her." Her mouth squared like a howling child's; then she began to beat her forehead with her hands.

"There you are, you see," said Miss Despenser.

"If you would only marry me!" said Hugh, and at once began to cloud the proposal with doubts and apologies. "I know so little about girls—no time to learn. I had to work so hard, and I've so little money. I'm awfully dull, I know. . . ."

"As dull as ditchwater," Miss Despenser said, but her remarks were now automatic. She had covered her retreat with them, and, exhausted with her efforts and her disappointment, could say no more. She took a pace back in the shadowy hall, and when at last Hugh stood up and helped Hester to do so she closed her eyes and could watch no longer.

"Good-bye," Hester said, turning to her. "I'm sorry, and thank you. I had better go back after all."

Miss Despenser kept her eyes shut; a hard tear was under each lid.

Hugh looked away from Hester for the first time and saw the old woman's wedge-shaped face, so angrily grieved, her down-turned mouth. With the palm of her hand she was pressing to her skirt the photograph of her dead sister. From his own timid loneliness he had knowledge of such a poverty of love. He said, "Thank you for taking care of her."

The tragic mask could not move, or the eyes open. When Hester and Hugh had gone she lifted her lids and two tears dropped out and made tracks down her face to her chin. She picked up the cat and wiped her wet face on his fur, then she gathered up the photographs and crammed them back into the mother-of-pearl-inlaid box.

Not long after, just as Mrs. Brimmer at the Hand and Flowers was saying, "Well, we choked her off, gentlemen," Miss Despenser entered the bar. "So sorry I am late. Some visitors called," she said cheerily.

"A pleasure, I'm sure," Mrs. Brimmer replied. "And now, last orders, if you please."

At the school Hester was enveloped by tact. Muriel, relieved at her reappearance, seemed unconcerned and talked of trivial things, though lapsing sometimes into sad preoccupation. Robert's lack of allusion was almost imbecilic. Hugh, suddenly masterful, had arranged with him that no words should pass, and they did not, although sometimes Hester felt swollen with the rehearsed explanations she was not allowed to make.

As day after day went by, poor little Mooney began at last to wonder if he had escaped expulsion; but Robert's abstracted ways prolonged the boys' uneasiness. Dissociation became the policy under this cloud—the copy of *Lady Chatterley's Lover*, or a Latin crib, lost its value; the shrubbery, or Hell's Kitchen, where they smoked, was deserted.

One day, after lunch, when Robert had said grace he still stood, as if he had more to say. They paused and turned their faces towards him, candid, innocent. Only Mooney looked down desperately at his plate—the five prune-stones at its edge: *this* year.

The announcement of Hugh's and Hester's engagement was a tremendous relief. Robert's attempt at joviality brought forth sycophantic cheers and smiles. They were all in a good humour, especially as one wedding present would do for both. "It is better for them not to marry outside people," the head boy explained. "Now what we want is for Matron to marry Mr. Wigmore!"

Hugh's first biology class of the afternoon was in a mood of refreshment and good humour.

"Congratulations, sir."

"Thank you, Palmer."

"Congratulations, sir."

"I will take Palmer as spokesman for all of you," Hugh said firmly. "Page fifty-one." They opened their books.

"So that's the solution," Beatrice said. "You were quite right to be patient and let things work their own way out."

"I don't know that I did that," Muriel said. "And it has taken a long time, and she hasn't gone yet."

"She seems too moony, too dull a girl to fall in love, be fallen in love with."

"Is love the prerogative of the bright ones? He is very dull himself, you know, and it is a good thing if two uninteresting people marry and keep their dullness to themselves. Though she has changed a little for the better—looks less *driven;* doesn't knock things over quite as much as she used; can sometimes drink a glass of water without spilling it."

"Well, if marriage stops her being clumsy it will be something." Then Beatrice asked slyly, "How has Robert taken it?"

"Nobly. He arranged Hugh's new job for him and still has nobody to take his place."

"I meant—about Hester."

"Oh, Hester!" Muriel's voice was light with annoyance. "I think I imagined a great deal of that." If Hester were going, her own agitation would sink; then she wanted her old life again, her picture of serene marriage, of Robert's devotion to her. She regretted having confided in Beatrice, who made past miseries more real by her knowledge of them. To turn the conversation she said, "I will give her a lovely wedding. I suppose that she has some friends she can invite—school friends, if nothing better. I have chosen the dress material. Just think, Beatrice, when *we* were married we wore those hideous short frocks. It would be our luck to strike that fashion. I wouldn't let anyone see my wedding photographs for all the world." With tender condescension they recalled the nineteen-twenties and the gay and gentle girlishness of their natures then.

Muriel began to feel energy and optimism as the holidays and the wedding grew nearer. She worked to bring to life one imagined scene, the beginning of peace for her; foresaw Hester and Hugh going down the steps to the car—"She was married from my house," she would tell people. "She was like a daughter to me"—and when the car had gone (forever, forever) down the drive, she and Robert would turn and go up the confetti-littered steps to begin their new—or, rather, their *old*—life, together and alone.

She worked on the wedding and discussed it incessantly. "Suppose it rains?" Robert said abruptly one night. Muriel was sitting up in bed while he undressed. She was brushing her hair and at his words parted it from her face, looked up at him in perplexity. "Are you angry about it, then?"

"Angry? I only said 'Suppose it rains?' "

"You sounded so sarcastic."

He got into bed and closed his eyes at once. Smoothing her hair back, she dropped the brush to the floor and put out the light. "You do love me, Robert?" she asked in her meekest voice.

"Yes, dear."

"You aren't still angry with me about Hester? It has turned out well in the end for her."

"I hope so."

"He will be very good to her, I am quite sure."

"Yes, I am sure too. Good night, Muriel."

"Good night, Robert."

He turned over and seemed to fall asleep; yet she doubted if he did so, and lay and listened for a long while to his regular, unbroken breathing. Once, to test him, she touched him gently with the back of her hand, but he did not turn to her as years ago he would have done. I cannot make him come to me, she thought in a panic. I cannot get my own way. She became wide awake with a longing for him to make love to her, to prove his need for her, so that she could claim his attention and so dominate him; but at last wished only to contend with her own desires, unusual and humiliating as they were to her. She lay close to him and masked her shame with a pretence of sleep. When he did not, would not, stir, her tenderness hardened to resentment. She raised herself and looked down at him. His profile was stern; his hair ruffled; he breathed steadily. He cannot be asleep, she thought as she bent over him, put her cheek to his brow, no longer dissembling or hiding her desire.

His stillness defeated her and after a while, hollowed and exhausted by her experience, she turned away and lay down on her side, listening to her thunderous heartbeat, feeling giddy. If I could be young again! she thought. If I could be young!

Two thrushes were singing in the garden before she fell asleep. The night had dishevelled her, her hair was tangled on the creased pillow, her body damp in the hot bed. But in her dreams a less disordered Muriel took command. She dreamed that she was making Hester's wedding cake—white and glistering it rose before her, a sacrificial cake, pagoda-shaped in tier on tier, with arcades of sugar pillars, garlanded friezes. Delicate as hoar-rimed ferns she made the fronded wreaths of flowers and leaves. It blossomed as she worked her magic on it with the splendid virtuosity of dreams. Yes, that is how it will be! she thought. And no one must ever touch it or break it. She had surprised herself with her own skill, and, standing back to view her work, felt assuaged, triumphant, but bereft too, as artists are when their work is done and gone for good.

The Short Stories

I Live in a World of Make-Believe

At the end of the village, the house, which was of a dazzling whiteness in summer, now stood sulphurous and dark against the snow, the plaster discoloured and flocky like ill-washed woollens, and the formal garden and the shrubbery a mass of strange humps. But none of this was without grandeur to Mrs. Miller, who fretted as she drew the curtains in her smaller house across the road.

Her view was across the lane and clean through the wrought-iron gates. Beyond these gates a life went on which absorbed and entranced her: the chauffeur brought his shining car to the front steps; a uniformed nanny emerged into the lane with the pram, from which white fur mittens vaguely waved; a bowed and earthy gardener threw maize over the frosty ground; and cockerels—magnificent with their glistering plumage, their crimson combs—danced forward savagely, printing their dagger-like tracks over the snow.

Symbols of all that seemed worth while in life passed and crossed on that gravelled courtyard—symbols of order and of plenty, of service, of the lesser devoted to the superior, and wages paid by the week; not, as Mrs. Miller paid her own charwoman, by the hour.

Since children make friends simply and quickly (being less on their dignity, less fearful of rebuff, than adults), in no time, as soon as the Millers moved in, their little boy had insinuated himself into the Big House, was riding the little girl's pony, had invaded nursery tea and even (for this he was scolded by his mother) Lady Luna's solitary breakfast. His mother scolded but listened to the description of Lady Luna pouring coffee for herself at one end of the cleared and deserted table at half-past nine of a morning, the white and red room rosy with a great fire, and, said Timmy Miller, "a good invention, a little cage on the table where you put bread in and it comes out toast."

"That's nothing," his mother said discontentedly. "Your granny has one just the same. And remember, I won't have you bothering over there at all hours of the day."

Then the telephone rang, and a light, inconsequential voice said, "Oh, you can't know me, my dear. I am Lady Luna from just across the road. We should so love it if you could come over for tea."

So the telephone bridged the narrow lane and dismissed for Mrs. Miller those intricacies of card-leaving she had often pondered in bed at night. She pondered many things at night, all those things that worried her—her husband, for instance, saying "front room" instead of "lounge" in the smaller house they had graduated from, and now her faint suspicion that "lounge" itself no longer did.

"I wish we had more books."

"Books?" he echoed, looking worried at once. "What for?"

"For all those built-in shelves. I'd like to call that room the library."

"What's it matter what it's called?"

"Books are such an expensive item, and I don't fancy them second-hand. You can't tell where they've been nor what they harbour."

"That's right," he agreed; for he always agreed—worried, depressed as they are, the husbands of ambitious women.

"And we ought to get an electric toaster. We waste bread"—she was using an argument he would like—"toasting it like that out in the kitchen."

He knew she would remain discontented forever, comparing life, as she did, with accounts of Edwardian house-parties she had read in novels; so that each day was wrong from the start, with its three boiled eggs instead of the great dishes on the sideboard (lifting one lid after another—the mushrooms, the devilled kidneys, the fish kedgeree—and casting remarks of great brilliance over one shoulder to those who sat at the table, slitting open with silver knives invitations to weddings, to garden parties and balls). That fantasy, in all her experience, was most nearly approached by the house across the road, and she lingered over drawing the curtains at teatime; so Lady Luna's voice on the telephone sent her hastening to her wardrobe to survey her potentialities.

While she painted her nails she assembled and had in readiness a few phrases against awkward pauses in the conversation—of which, had she known, there would be none with Lady Luna, whose murmurings were gentle and continuous like those of doves in summer. For Lady Luna asked questions which she did not intend should be answered; she cooed, murmured, and agreed; without sympathy, she uttered sympathetic phrases; and always her eyes had a flitting, heedless restlessness, like the darting, purposeless motions of little fishes.

In the shadow of all this her child, Constance, sat still and unperturbed—looking well bred, no doubt, thought Mrs. Miller, deprived of her chosen phrases; well bred, but plain, colourless, and straight-haired; not cute, as she would have liked a little girl of her own to be.

Mrs. Miller felt insulted by the flowing, indifferent talk of her hostess and by the tea itself, over which no trouble had been expended. She felt vaguely that had she also been titled, the cake would have contained cream, not knowing that if the Queen of England herself (a phrase she often used) had been expected, the same dry little rock buns with their swollen, burned currants would have been proffered.

After tea Nanny brought in the baby and proved a better hostess than her mistress, with her compliments on Timmy Miller's good colour; and what a pity Constance did not fill out in the same way, she said, and then, dandling the vaguely stamping, whimpering baby, her fingers in his closed fists, astonished Mrs. Miller, who did not talk often to nannies, by saying, "We're a little constipated today, I'm afraid, and that makes us fretty and cross. We shall have to try a spoonful of the prune purée at bedtime. Shan't we, darling?" The baby put his feet down emphatically but without control; his chin was wet with dribble, and his eyes stared.

Meanwhile Lady Luna had lapsed into a drowsy silence, as if, her murmurings done, she waited only for her guest to go. Her carefully tended but worn-out little face looked still and empty.

Manners! thought Mrs. Miller, her colour rising. Only her son—and children have their own private agonies—noted this.

"And you are sure you will not have a sherry?" Lady Luna asked suddenly in the hall. "For the road," she added, pleased with the contemporary phraseology she acquired so spasmodically and used too late.

That evening there was nothing of all Lady Luna's talk that Mrs. Miller could remember or pass on to her husband when he came home. He had brought the electric toaster for the sake of peace and quiet, but even that fact could not smooth out the gathers on her brow.

"Did you have a nice tea?" he asked at last.

She made a bitter, scoffing noise, and presently said, "Buns I'd not hand to a charwoman."

"Then you will have to put her to shame with some of your nice confections," he said gently, tenderly jocular, as if to a sick and peevish child.

"I'm not likely to ask her. Timmy, it's your bedtime."

The little boy looked up from his game, the dice rattling still in the egg-cup in his hand. This rather grubby little hand was dreadfully pathetic, his father suddenly decided. "Good night, old chap," he said kindly.

The boy looked strained, his eyes widened by tears he could scarcely keep back. "Why? Why won't you ask her?" he began.

Mrs. Miller reached for a piece of embroidery, and her husband thought that the only time she appeared relaxed or casual was when she was working herself up into a great storm of anger. She chose a strand of green silk and began to embroider an eye in a peacock's tail. The three of them watched and listened to the needle passing through the linen.

"Your mother," said Mrs. Miller quietly, and as if she were not talking of herself, "has no cook, nor house-parlour-maid, nor nanny. . . ."

They waited still.

"She has only herself," she continued, "to scrub the floors and bake . . ."

She produced a formidable vision of vast flagged floors and great bread ovens, her husband thought.

". . . and wash and mend," she concluded. She drew her needle out to the length of the silk and, looking up at them, smiled bravely.

"But doesn't Mrs. Wilson do the scrubbing?" Mr. Miller asked, as if to erase this picture of intolerable human suffering.

He could not understand the intricacies of housewifery, Mrs. Miller implied by her brief look and her silence.

"But—"

"Yes, Timmy?"

"I wish—"

"Don't stammer, dear. Would you like shredded wheat for your supper?"

"Yes, please."

Dreadful, his father thought, seeing a child biding his time, trying to weather his mother's caprice and bitterness. Too young to be learning worldly wisdom, that unengaging quality.

Mrs. Miller, like a good mother, laid aside her embroidery

and went to see her child to bed. His father could not help him. The boy went quietly away to his shredded wheat.

Yet *she* suffers too, Mr. Miller suddenly thought. *We* suffer because of *her* suffering. Whatever she lacks in life, whatever she fails to grasp, *we* pay for. For himself, he no longer cared, but he did not like to see his little boy going to bed so quietly, with his requests weighing heavily in him until a suitable occasion for cajolery arose.

When Mrs. Miller came back he wanted to say to her, "Let me show you something true for one moment. Let me help you look into your son's heart, or your own even. And if you are always to measure your condition against other people's, let it not be forever against people who do not exist. For life will never be what you have imagined. Not for five minutes even."

As a girl she had been affected. "I live in a world of make-believe," she would laugh, boastfully, as one laughs when confessing to well-loved weaknesses.

He said nothing. He watched her unhappy eyes and mouth as she sewed. Then it occurred to him that all the time she really intended asking Lady Luna and the child to tea, that she was making a weapon of her reluctance so that she might drive them all to a frenzy with it when the time came. He could not determine how he knew this, but years of living with her had shown him that none of the simple, obvious things about her was true (her calmness covered fury, her fury was deliberately indulged and delighted in), so that when he saw the forthright he looked at once much deeper than that and through mazes of deception came usually to the reverse.

As she sewed, her eyes darted often to one thing after

another in the room, and he thought that she must be measuring these things with the eyes of Lady Luna, who might see them thus if she came to tea. She seemed to dwell most upon those shelves where once the people of the house had kept their books, and where now china was carefully spaced out—but with a poor effect, it could not be denied.

The next day he brought home a row of old sermons bound in calf and gilded richly. She was pleased, and for once allowed herself to show her pleasure. "I dare say they're quite clean, and it isn't as if we shall be reading them. I've always said books are the making of a room." And her eyes travelled to the next empty shelf, along which she rearranged some china.

So Mr. Miller began to collect books—sets of books with heavily gilded spines, in calf, in marbled paper, to tone in with the room, which slowly came to look, Mrs. Miller said, more like a library every day. Coming home in the train he would even dip into these volumes and read a little, but the long *f*s worried him and tried his patience.

"I suppose I must ask that woman over one day sometime," she said one evening, and although her voice was fretful, her eyes rested with satisfaction on her cosy room. "What about asking them for sherry?"

At once he could foresee how poor Timmy would be hastened into bed, nagged at and scolded, then later, to make up for it, allowed to sit up with a plateful of pieces from the snacks, rejected from downstairs, broken cheese straws and scorched almonds.

"It would be nice for Timmy to have the little girl to tea," he began, as she had known he would.

"I won't have people to tea while I have to carry in my

own teapot," she cried. Her voice rang tragically as she envisaged this disgrace.

He knew that another man would have laughed, but there was no laughter left in him because his son was involved.

One of his friends had put his head in a gas oven and come by a peaceful end that way. This incident had made a great impression upon Mr. Miller, who imagined in every detail himself doing the same thing. You could make it quite comfortable with a cushion, he now thought. Just be relaxed, breathe deeply, not fight against it, pretend you're at the dentist's without that hateful spinning back into consciousness with the taste of blood in your mouth and the voice saying, "Rinse, please."

"What are you thinking?" his wife suddenly asked.

"About the dentist, dear."

"Well, I can't see anything to smile about in that," she said restlessly, and she threw aside her library book, which was morbid.

In the morning she telephoned Lady Luna to ask her to tea at the end of the week.

"But how lovely!" cried Lady Luna. "Constance will be delighted."

Her rapturous acceptance was overdone, Mrs. Miller thought. In one who obviously had far more exciting engagements, this enthusiasm seemed automatic, even absent-minded. But Timmy went to school happy the next day, and Mrs. Miller called in the sweep so that she could be sure the chimney would not smoke.

On Thursday she did not sit down all day, she told her husband in the evening. She was a great one for not sitting down all day, not touching a morsel of food, never sleeping a wink all night and hearing every quarter of an hour strike from midnight until dawn.

In the larder tiny éclairs and meringues cooled on wire trays, silver was polished, apple jelly spooned carefully into cut glass, rosettes of pink icing piped onto the middle of biscuits. Two branches of white lilac stood leafless in a jar under the sink—the coolest, safest place—and were given an aspirin tablet every time Mrs. Miller thought of it. The drawn-thread traycloth was dipped into sugar and water and ironed damp.

"You'll be too worn out by tomorrow to enjoy yourself," Mr. Miller observed as he drank tinned soup.

"I don't expect to enjoy myself," his wife replied, for once truthful. "I've got a splitting head."

"Well, have some supper, old girl."

"I couldn't bring myself to. And Robert, I do wish you wouldn't call me 'old girl.' Even when we're by ourselves. It isn't very kind." Her mouth drooped, her voice quivered.

"I meant it kindly. Have a drop of gin."

"Of course not. You know I only drink in company. To be sociable. I don't really care for it at all, the taste is so nasty. I can't understand people going so mad over it, when it's so expensive too. Think what you could do with the money."

He couldn't really think of anything, so he went on with his soup.

"Oh, my back's breaking," she continued. "What with leaning over that bath washing Timmy, and then the sink all day . . ." He scarcely listened. Her head was splitting and her back was breaking, and, still wearing an apron, she perched for a moment on the arm of a chair and cheered him on as he ate his supper.

"She ought to have gone on the stage," he thought. "She'd have had them crying their eyes out."

She was late to bed. She put her hair into curlers and creamed her hands; then, wearing a pair of cotton gloves, got into bed and lay there, twitching slightly with fatigue, and going back over the day's work and forward over to-morrow's. As she took it for granted that her husband was lying beside her doing the same, she felt no hesitation in making her observations aloud from time to time.

Yet in spite of the hell she had made of the house for two days, when Timmy came from school next day at half-past three he found his mother good-humoured and at ease, the worst over, wearing her best shoes, but a tweed suit which would show Lady Luna that she regarded the occasion as of little importance. He was warmed by her good humour, responding at once to her mood with the intolerable sensitivity of those who live with the quick-tempered. He inspected with Constance's eyes the little biscuits, the pale meringues. Two of the best apple logs were laid on the bright fire. The lilac was seen to be magnificent now that it had been taken from under the sink, and the rows of books looked as if they had been in the family for years.

Mrs. Miller stood by the window, feeling like a good producer who knows that every detail has been attended to, every difficulty foreseen, and who can await the lifting of the curtain with confidence and even pleasure.

"I wish it could always be like this," thought Timmy vaguely.

And then—it was twenty to four—the gate creaked and Auntie Flo appeared with little Valerie and came, waving and calling, up the path.

Across the road Nanny was rinsing out pillow-slips in Sanitas. At twelve that morning, just as the music mistress arrived, Constance, practising scales in the schoolroom, paled and then vomited all over the piano and into her lap.

While Nanny sponged the keys and changed Constance's blouse and skirt, Lady Luna took Miss Hayday, who was fond of painting, to see a Gainsborough of her great-great-grandmother in the drawing room.

Constance, so suddenly ill, was quite as suddenly restored, and it would be a pity, her mother said, to have brought Miss Hayday from one end of the village to another for nothing. So, a little late, they sat down to the lesson, in a room still smelling rather of sick, only partly covered up by disinfectant, and Constance, in a clean blouse, started off on her arpeggios, her tongue between her lips, her straight hair falling forward over her shoulders, and Miss Hayday, sitting beside her on an upright chair, breathing in a panic-stricken way into a little scented handkerchief.

Afterwards Constance ate a good lunch, and while she did so her mother remarked a great deal on the way children are down one moment and up the next. After this Constance went to lie on her bed with a book, and very soon was sick again, this time all over the pink eiderdown.

Auntie Flo was Mr. Miller's sister, and she had come on the bus with an oilcloth bag containing a dozen eggs and a jar of pickled cabbage. She seemed so very pleased to see her sister-in-law and called, "Yoo-hoo," through the letter-box, always being full of high spirits.

"Oh, God, how couldst Thou?" Mrs. Miller cried in silent

anguish as she opened the door. Her world swayed and crashed at the thought of mingling together Auntie Flo and Lady Luna. Even her neck was flushed as she gave her cheek to be kissed, and Timmy watched her with anxiety.

Auntie Flo never talked, she always shouted, and she shouted now. "Take them eggs into the scullery for your auntie, Valerie. No, leave your pixie on, that's a good girl. She's had the ringworm. All over now, of course, but the hair doesn't seem to grow very quick. Never mind. Well, this is lovely, dear. A lovely home."

Mrs. Miller had begun to sweat. One absurd excuse after another for getting rid of Auntie Flo swept through her panic-confused mind—such as taking her to one side and saying she awaited the doctor ("They suspect a touch of cancer"), or a lover, or children with diphtheria coming to tea. While she thought, she smiled frostily at Valerie and glanced continually towards the window.

Valerie sat on the edge of a chair, swinging her legs and fidgeting with a loose tooth, and she seemed to have the smirk on her of a child who knows she is the apple of her mother's eye.

Auntie Flo rattled on. "And although I say it, she really does talk lovely since she went to the private school. It's worth every penny of the money, not a penny of it would I begrudge them, the lovely way she talks now. My next-door neighbour, she said to me only yesterday, 'Mrs. Shaw,' she said, 'doesn't your Valerie talk lovely now she goes to the private school? I was saying to Will last night,' she said, 'doesn't young Valerie next door talk lovely, you'd never credit it . . .' "

Mrs. Miller, her throat choked with tears, looked out of

the window, wringing her hands. "I must get rid of her. I must get rid of her. In five more minutes she must be out of this house, and her horrifying little Valerie with her."

At half-past five Lady Luna lowered the bound volume of *Little Folks* she had had as a child and stopped reading aloud in the middle of the story.

"Oh, my God!" she said to Constance, who was now properly in bed, eating arrowroot mould. "We ought to've gone to tea across the road. I'll have to telephone."

"Oh, not till the bottom of the page," Constance wailed, taking advantage of her indisposition.

Her mother agreed without argument, for the story lulled her nerves with beautiful nostalgia for her own cosy childhood, when nobody had ever heard of the Labour government, and servants were grateful for their jobs.

Timmy lay still, too rigid with apprehension to draw his cold feet up into a warmer place in the bed. Downstairs his parents quarrelled. They quarrelled all the time Mrs. Miller was getting supper; the dissenting voices swelled or diminished as doors were opened or closed, and the argument went on from room to room.

"You let my own sister go away without even a cup of tea," cried Mr. Miller, "after her coming all that way to see you, out of the kindness of her heart."

"The child had ringworm. She had no business to have come."

"You know full well you let her go because you're such a bloody snob; she wasn't good enough to meet her ladyship—"

"How dare you swear at me!"

"It's just about time someone did, to knock some sense into your empty head. Damn fine friends, too, without the manners of a—"

"Don't shout!"

"I'll shout as much as I bloody well please." He became exhilarated with his success. He had never answered her back before, and she was frightened, he could see.

Her head wheeled and hammered. She sat down at the table with her arms before her and put her head down on them and began to cry.

The thought of Timmy's hearing this deflated Mr. Miller. He put a hand on her shoulder, hoping to steady her.

"Poor old Flo," he conceded. "I suppose she is a bit of a rough diamond."

"It was the ringworm," Mrs. Miller sobbed into her sleeve.

"All right. All right. Let's get on with some supper and have a nice quiet sit-down by the fire."

"I don't know what to have for supper." For her plans had not extended beyond teatime.

"Well, we can make do with something—a bit of cold meat out there, and a nice jar of pickled cabbage, I saw. That'll be a change. Now don't go off again. What's the matter now? The boy'll hear you."

She went out into the kitchen and held her handkerchief under the cold water and then put it to her aching forehead.

"And there's all these nice cakes," her tactless husband went on. "We can follow up with some of these."

"All right," she said meekly.

His very air was one of mastery and decision; even cutting

his meat, forking pickled cabbage onto his plate, he seemed different, she thought.

She was very subdued. She ate nothing, her head ached so. When the telephone rang she started and began to tremble.

There was the cool, inconsequential voice. "My dear, it's Winifred Luna, I know you will never forgive me. We've had such a day—Constance vomiting the whole time, and Cook's afternoon off—it simply is one thing after another with children, they're up one minute and down the next. What Nanny and I have had to put up with this day—but now she has had an enormous amount of arrowroot mould and gone fast to sleep, like a baby—though my babies were never so marvellous as all that about sleeping—and Nanny and I are just exhausted—and on top of it all the dreadful feeling that you are not going to forgive my rudeness and thoughtlessness, but I expect you will be very understanding and give us just one more chance. Perhaps we could pop over tomorrow instead . . ."

"Of course," said Mrs. Miller faintly, and smiled wanly into the telephone.

"Then that will be lovely. Constance will be so delighted. It will quite cheer her up."

When Mrs. Miller put down the receiver she went on standing there, her eyes closed, her wrist to her brow, her mouth dragged tragically down. "Sarah Bernhardt," thought her husband, eating one éclair after another.

Spry Old Character

The Home for the Blind absorbed the surplus of that rural charity so much more pleasant to give than to receive—the cakes left over from the Women's Institute party, and concerts which could no longer tempt appetites more than satisfied by homely monologues and the postmistress's zither. Fruit and vegetables from the Harvest Festival seemed not richer from their blessing but vitiated by being too much arranged, too much stared at. The bread in the shape of a corn sheaf tasted of incense, and, with its mainly visual appeal, was wasted on the blind.

No week went by without some dispiriting jollity being forced upon them. This week it was a choir of schoolgirls singing "Orpheus with His Lute." Which drives me finally up the wall, Harry decided, and clapped his great horny hands together at the end with relief. "Your *nails*, Harry!" Matron had said earlier, as if he were a child; and, like a child, he winced each time the scissors touched him. "You've been biting them again. I shall have to get very cross with you." He imagined her irritating smile: false teeth like china, no doubt; thin lips. He had been on the wrong side of her from the start; had asked her to read out to him the runners at Newmarket. "You old terror! I shall do nothing of the kind. I'm not having that sort of thing here." He was helpless. Reading by touch he regarded as a miracle and beyond him. He had steered clear of books when he could see, and they held even less attraction now that tedious lessons as well as indifference stood in the way; and the *Sporting Life* was not set in Braille, he soon discovered.

His request had scandalized, for, he had soon decided, only the virtuous lose their sight—perhaps as a further test of their saintly patience. None of his friends in London—the Boys—had ever known such a calamity, and rebelliousness, as if at some clerical error, hardened his heart. Set down in this institution after his sister's death, he was a fish out of water. I'm just not the type, he thought, over and over again.

What Harry called the rural setup—the great house in its park, the village, the surrounding countryside—was visually unimaginable to him. His nearest experience of it was Hampstead Heath or the view (ignored) from Goodwood Race Course. Country to him was negative—simply a place where there was not a town. The large rooms of the Home unnerved him. In his sister's parlor he could not go far wrong, edging round the table which took up most of the space; and the heat from the fire, the clock ticking on the dresser, had given him his bearings. After she died he was helpless. The Home had appealed to him as a wonderful alternative to his own picture of himself out in the street with a tray of matches and a card pinned to his breast with some words such as "On My Beam Ends" or, simply, "Blind."

"You'll have the company of others like you," his neighbors had told him. This was not so. He found himself in a society whose existence he had never, in his old egotism, contemplated, and whose ways soon lowered his vitality. He had nothing in common with these faded seamstresses, the prophet-like lay preacher, an old piano tuner who believed he was the reincarnation of Beethoven—with elderly people who had lived more than half a dim lifetime in dark drapers' shops in country towns. They almost might not have been blind, even, for they found their way about the house, its grounds, the village, with pride and confidence. Indoors they bickered about the wireless—for the ladies liked a nice domestic play and thought some of the variety programs "suggestive." The racing results were always switched to something different hastily, before they could contaminate the air.

"I once went to a race meeting," Miss Arbuthnot admitted. She had been a governess in Russia in the czarist days and had taken tea with Rasputin. Now she overrode her companions with her past grandeur. No one knew, perhaps she least of all, what bizarre experience might be related next. "It was at Ascot after the last war. I mean the one before that. I went as chaperon to Lady Allegra Faringdon and one of the Ponsonby cousins."

"Did you see the King and Queen drive down the course?" asked the sycophantic Mrs. Hussey. "What a picture that must be!"

"It is quite a pageant of English life. The cream of the cream, as one might say. But dear, dear me! What a tiring way to spend a day! My poor feet! I wore some pale grey buckskin shoes, and how they *drew!* I daresay they would look very old-fashioned nowadays, but then they were quite *à la.*" She gave her silvery, trilling laugh. "Well, I have been once. I know what it is like, and I know that I give the preference to Henley, even if the crowd there is not so brilliant. Oh, yes, give me Henley any day."

No one would be likely to give her any such thing ever again, but this occurred only to Harry.

"Did you have any luck—with the horses, I mean?" he asked, breaking his sullen silence with his coarse, breathy voice. Exasperation and nostalgia forced him to speak, although to do so invited ridicule. He was driven to broach the subject as lovers are often driven to mention the beloved's name, even in casual conversation with unworthy people.

"Do you mean betting?"

"What else do you go for?" he asked huffily.

"Well, certainly not for that, I hope. For the spectacle, the occasion—a brilliant opening to the London season."

No one thought—their indignation was so centered upon Harry—that she spoke less as a governess than as a duchess. She coloured their lives with her extravagances, whereas Harry only underlined their plight; stumbling, cursing, spilling food, he had brought the word "blindness" into their midst and was a threat to their courage.

Cantankerous old virgin, he thought. Trying to come it over me. A spinster to him was a figure of fun, but now he, not she, sat humble and grumpy and rejected.

The evening of the concert Miss Arbuthnot, with the advantage of her cultured life behind her ("Ah! Chaliapin in *Boris!* After that, one is never quite the same person again"), sat in the front row and led and tempered the applause. A humorous song in country dialect wound up the evening, and her fluting laugh gave the cue for broad-minded appreciation. Then chairs scraped back and talk broke out. Harry tapped his way to a corner and sat there alone.

The girls, told to mingle, to bring their sunshine into these dark lives, began nervously to hand round buns, unsure of how far the blind could help themselves. They were desperately tactful. ("I made the most frightful *faux pas*," they would chatter in the bus going home. "Dropped the most appalling brick. Wasn't it all depressing? Poor old things! But it doesn't bear thinking of, of course.")

One girl obediently came towards Harry. "Would you like a cake?"

"That's very kind of you, missie."

She held the plate out awkwardly, but he made no movement towards it.

"Shall I— May I give you one?"

"I should maybe knock them all on the floor if I start feeling about," he said gloomily.

She put a cake into his hand, and as the crumbs began to fall on his waistcoat and knees she looked away, fearing that he might guess the direction of her glance, for she had been told that the blind develop the other senses to an uncanny degree.

Her young voice was a pleasure to him. He was growing used to voices either elderly or condescending. Hoping to detain her a little longer, he said, "You all sang very nice indeed."

"I'm so glad you enjoyed it."

He thought: I'd only have run a mile from it, given half a chance.

"I'm fond of a nice voice," he said. "My mother was a singer."

"Oh, really?" She had not intended to sound so incredulous, but her affectation of brightness had grown out of hand.

"She was a big figure on the halls—in more ways than just the one. A fine great bust and thighs she had, but small feet. Collins' Music Hall and the Met. I daresay you heard of them?"

"I can't really say I have."

"She had her name on the bills—Lottie Throstle. That was her stage name, and a funny, old-fashioned name it must sound nowadays, but you used to have to have something out of the usual run. Louie Breakspear her real name was. I expect you've heard your mum and dad speak of Lottie Throstle."

"I can't remember—"

"She was a good old sort." (She'd have had you taped, he thought. I can hear her now: "Ay can't say, Ay'm sure.") " 'Slip Round the Corner, Charlie,' that was her song. Did you ever hear that one?" ("No, Ay can't say Ay hev," he answered for her. No, I thought not. Orpheus and his sodding lute's more your ticket.)

"No, I haven't." She glanced desperately about her.

"What colour dress you got on, miss?"

"White."

"Well, don't be shy! Nothing wrong with a white dress at your age. When you're fat and forty I should advise thinking twice about it. You all got white dresses on?"

"Yes."

Must look like the Virgins' Outing, he thought. What a sight! Never came my way, of course, before now. No one ever served up twenty-five virgins in white to me in those days. Showing common sense on their part, no doubt.

His rough hand groped forward and rasped against her silk frock. "That's nice material! I like nice material. My sister Lily who died was a dressmaker." The girl, rigid, turned her head sharply aside. He smelled the sudden sweat of fear and embarrassment on her skin and drew back his hand.

"Now, young lady, we can't let you monopolize Mr. Breakspear," Matron said, coming swiftly across the room. "Here's Miss Wilcox to have a chat with you, Harry. Miss Wilcox is the choir mistress. She brings the girls here every year to give us this wonderful experience. You know, Miss Wilcox, Harry is quite the naughtiest of all my old darlings. He thinks we treat him so badly. Oh, yes, you do, Harry. You grumble from morning till night. And so lazy! Such a lovely basket he was going to make, but he lost all interest in it in next to no time."

Sullenly he sat beside Miss Wilcox. When coffee was brought to him, he spilled it purposely. He had no pride in overcoming difficulties, as the others had. His waistcoat was evidence of this. He was angry that Matron had mentioned his basketwork, for a very deep shame had overtaken him when they tried to teach him such a craft. He saw a picture of his humiliation, as if through his friends' eyes—the poor old codger, broken, helpless, back to the bottom class at school. "You want to be independent," the teacher had said, seeing him slumped there, idle with misery. He thought they did not understand the meaning of the word.

"You haven't been here long?" Miss Wilcox inquired kindly.

"No, only since my sister Lily died. I went to live along

with her when I lost my wife. I've been a widower nineteen years now. She was a good old sort, my wife."

"I'm sure she was."

Why's she so sure, he wondered, when she never as much as clapped eyes on her? She could have been a terrible old tartar for all she knows.

But he liked to talk and none of the others would ever listen to him. He engaged Miss Wilcox, determined to prevent her escaping. "I lost my sight three years ago, on account of a kick I had on the head from a horse. I used to be a horse dealer at one time." Then he remembered that no one spoke about being blind. This apparently trivial matter was never discussed.

"How very interesting!"

"I made a packet of money in those days. At one time I was a driver on the old horse buses. You could see those animals dragging up Highgate Hill with their noses on the ground nearly. I bought an old mare off of them for a couple of quid, and turned her out on a bit of grass I used to rent. Time I'd fed her up and got her coat nice with dandelion leaves and clover, I sold her for twenty pounds. Everything I touched went right for me in those days. She was the one who kicked me on the head. Francie, we called her. I always wished I could tell the wife what the doctors said. If I'd have said to her, 'You know, Florrie, what they hold Francie did to me all those years ago?' she would never have believed me. But that's what they reckoned. Delayed action they reckoned it was."

"Extraordinary!" Miss Wilcox murmured.

"Now, you old chatterbox!" Matron said. "We're going to sing 'Jerusalem' all together before the girls go home. And none of your nonsense, Harry. He's such an old rascal about hymns, Miss Wilcox."

Once he had refused to join in, believing that hymn-singing was a matter of personal choice, and not *his* choice. Now he knew that the blind are always religious, as they are cheerful, industrious, and independent. He no longer argued but stood up clumsily, feet apart, hands clasped over his paunch, and moved his lips feebly until the music stopped.

In the first weeks of his blindness he had suffered attacks of hysteria as wave upon wave of terror and frustration swept across him. "Your language!" his sister would say, her hand checking the wheel of the sewing machine. "Why don't we go round to the Lion for a beer?" She would button up his overcoat for him, saying, "I can't bear to see you fidgeting with your clothes." He would put on his old bowler hat, and, arm in arm, they would go along the street. "Good evening, Mrs. Simpson. That was Mrs. Simpson went by, Harry." She used no tact or Montessori methods on him. In the pub she would say, "Mind out, you! Let Harry sit down. How would *you* like to be blind?" They were all glad to see him. They read out the winners and prices for him. He knew the scene so well that he had no need to look at it, and the sensation of panic would be eased from him.

Now a deeper despair showed him daily the real tragedy of his blindness. This orderly, aseptic world was not only new to him but beyond his imagining. Food and talk had lost their richness. Central heating provided no warmth; he crouched over radiators with his hands spread over the pipes, his head aching with the dryness of the air. No one buttoned his coat for him. He tapped his way round with his stick, often hitting out viciously and swearing. "There are ladies present," he was told, and, indeed, this was so. They lowered the atmosphere with little jealousies and edged remarks, and irritated with their arguments about birds ("I could not mistake a chaffinch's song, Mrs. Hussey, being country bred and born") or about royalty ("But both Lady Mary *and* Lady May Cambridge were bridesmaids to the Duchess of York"). They always remembered as if it were yesterday, although begging pardon for contradicting. Morale was very high, as it so often is in a community where tragedy is present. Harry was reminded of the blitz, and Cockney resilience and understatement. Although a Cockney himself, he detested understatement. Some Irish strain in him allowed his mind to dwell on the mournful, to spread alarm and despondency, and to envisage with clarity the possibilities of defeat. When he confessed to fear, the Boys had relished the joke. "That'll be the day!" they had said. He had found the burden of their morale very tiring. The war's bad enough in itself, he had thought; as now he thought, Surely it's bad enough being blind, when he was expected to sing hymns and alter all his ways as well.

After the concert, his luck changed; at first, though, it seemed to deteriorate. The still, moist winter weather drew the other inmates out on walks about the village. Only Miss Arbuthnot remained indoors with a slight cold. In the end, the sense of nervousness and irritation she induced in Harry drove him out too. He wandered alone, a little scared, down the drive and out onto the highroad. He followed the brick wall along and turned with it into a narrow lane with a soft surface.

The hedges dripped with moisture, although it was not raining. All about that neighbourhood there was a resinous scent in the air, which was pronounced healthy by Matron, who snuffed it up enthusiastically, as if she were a war horse smelling battle. Harry's tread was now muffled by pine needles, and a fir cone dropped on his shoulder, startling him wretchedly. Every sound in the hedgerow unnerved him; he imagined small bright-eyed animals watching his progress. From not following the curve of the hedge sharply enough, he ran his face against wet hawthorn twigs. He felt giddiness, as if he were wandering in a circle. Bad enough being out by myself in the country, let alone being blind too, he thought as he stumbled in a rut.

He could imagine Matron when he returned—if he returned. "Why, Harry, you naughty old thing, going off like that! Why didn't you go with Mr. Thomas, who knows the neighbourhood so well and could have told you the names of all the birds you heard, and made it nice and interesting!"

The only birds he, Harry, could recognize—and he did not wish to recognize any—were jackdaws (and they were really rooks), who seemed to congregate above him through his walk, wheeling and cawing in an offensive manner; perhaps disputing over him, he thought morbidly, staking their claims before he dropped.

Then suddenly he lost hedge and ditch. He was treading on turf, and the air had widened. He felt a great space about him and the wind blowing, as if he were on a sea cliff, which he knew he could not be in Oxfordshire. With a sense of being confronted by an immense drop—a blind man's vertigo—he dared not take a pace forward but stood swaying a little, near to tears.

He heard rough breathing, and a large dog jumped upon him. In terror, he thrashed about with his stick, the tears now pouring from his eyes, which had no other function.

He heard a woman's voice calling and the squelch of the wet turf as she ran towards him across what he had imagined to be the middle of the air. She beat the dog away and took Harry's arm. "You all right, dear? He's plastered you up properly, but it'll brush off when it's dry."

"I don't know where I am," Harry said, fumbling for his handkerchief.

"It's the common where the bus stops." She pulled his handkerchief from his pocket and gave it to him. "That's our bus over there."

"You a conductress, then?"

"That's right, dear. You're from that Home, are you? It's on the route and we can give you a lift."

"I don't have any coppers on me."

"You needn't worry about that. Just take my arm and we're nearly there. It's a scandal the way they let you wander about."

"The others manage better nor I. I'm not one for the country. It always gives me the wind up."

At the gates of the Home she helped him down, saying, "Any time, dear. Only too pleased. Take care of yourself. Bye-bye!"

No one had noticed his absence, and he concealed his adventure. One of the daily cleaners, with whom he felt more confidence than with the resident staff, brushed his coat for him.

After this the lane that had held such terror was his escape route. The buses came every hour, and he would sometimes be waiting there or the drivers would see him stumbling across the common and would sound the horn in welcome. Sitting in the bus before it drew out, he could enjoy the only normal conversation of his day.

"A shilling each way Flighty Frances! That's not much for a man of your substance, Harry."

"It's just I fancy the name. I had an old mare of the name of Francie. Time was, no doubt, I'd have had a fiver on it. Now I'm left about as free of money as a toad of fleas."

He tried to roll his own cigarettes, but tore the paper and spilled the tobacco until the bus drivers learned to help him. In their company he opened out, became garrulous, waggish, his old manner returning. He came to know one driver from another and to call each by his name. Their camaraderie opened up to him garage gossip, feuds at the depot, a new language, a new life. His relationship with them was not one of equality, for they had too much to give and he nothing. This he sensed, and while taking their badinage and imagining their winks, he played up his part—the lowering role of a proper old character—and extracted what he could from it, even to the extent of hinting and scrounging. His fumblings with his cigarette-making became more piteous than was necessary.

"Oh, for goodness' sake, have a proper cigarette—messing about like that."

"That's all I got the lolly for, mate."

"Whose fault's that—if you've got to drink yourself silly every night?"

"I haven't had a pint since I came down here."

"Well, where's your money gone to? Wild living, I suppose. And women."

"Now, don't you start taking the mike out of me, Fred." He used their names a great deal; the first pride he had felt since his blindness was in distinguishing Fred from Syd or Lil from Marg. The women had more individuality to him, with wider variety of inflection and vocabulary and tone, and the different scents of their powder and their hair.

"Supposing Flighty Frances comes in, what are you going to do with your winnings, Harry? Take us all out for a beer?"

"I'll do that," he said. "I forget the taste of it myself. I could do with a nice brown. It's the price of it, though, and how to find my way back afterwards, and all them old codgers sitting round fanning theirselves each time I free a belch. Very offhand they can be with their ways."

"What do you do all day?"

The driver felt a curiosity about a life so different from his own, imagined a workhouse with old people groping about, arms extended, as if playing blindman's buff.

"We have a nice listen to the wireless set—a lot of music which I never liked the sound of anyway, and plays about sets of people carrying on as if they need their backside kicked. You never met a breed of people like these customers on the wireless; what they get into a rare consternation about is nobody's business. Then we might have some old Army gent give a talk about abroad and the rum ways they get into over there, but personally I've got my own troubles, so I lie back and get in a bit of shut-eye. One night we had a wagonload of virgins up there singing hymns."

He played to the gallery, which repaid him with cigarettes and bonhomie. His repartee became so strained that sometimes he almost waited to hear Florrie, his late wife, say sharply, "That's enough now, Harry. It's about time we heard something from someone else." He had always talked too much; was a bad listener—almost a non-listener, for he simply waited without patience for others to stop talking so that he might cap their story. Well, hurry up, hurry up, he would think. Get a move on with it, man. I got something to say myself on those lines. If you go drivelling on much longer, chances are I'll forget it.

"No, what I'd do—say this horse comes in, bar the fact I'd only make about seven bob all told—but what I'd do is take the bus down to the fair on Saturday. I like a nice lively fair."

"What, and have a go on the coconut shies?"

"I wouldn't mind, Fred," he boasted.

"You can come along with me and Charlie, Saturday evening," Fred said, adding with an ungraciousness he did not intend, "Makes no odds to us."

"Well, I don't know," Harry said. "Have to see what's fixed up for Saturday. I'll let you know tomorrow."

"All right, Harry. We'll get one of the boys to pick you up at the gates Saturday after tea, and we can put you on the last bus along with all those coconuts you're going to knock down."

The bus was stopped at the gates for him. He lifted his white stick in farewell and then walked up the drive, slashing out at the rhododendron hedge and whistling shrilly. Now he was in for a spell of his old difficulty—currying favour.

He would not have admitted to Fred that he could not come and go as he pleased, that for the rest of the day he must fawn on Matron and prepare his request.

This he overdid, as a child would, arousing suspicion and lowering himself in his own eyes. He praised the minced meat and went into ecstasies over the prunes and custard. His unctuous voice was a deep abasement to him and an insult to Matron's intelligence.

"My, that's what I call a meal, quite a prewar touch about it. Now say I have another go at that basketwork, ma'am?"

"What are you up to today, Harry?"

"Me?"

"Yes, you."

Later the wind drove gusts of fair music up the hill. Miss Arbuthnot complained, but Harry could not hear the music. Missing so much that the others heard was an added worry to him lately, for to lose hearing as well would finish him as a person. It would leave him at the mercy of his own thoughts, which had always bored him. His tongue did his thinking for him. Other people's talk struck words from him like a light from a match. His phrases were quick and ready-made and soon forgotten, but he feared a silence and they filled it.

Matron found him alone, after the basketmaking class was over. He was involved in a great tangle of withies. His enormous hands, ingrained with dirt, looked so ill-adapted to the task that Matron, stringent as she was about the difficulties of others, found them wretchedly pathetic. So few men of action came her way; the burly, the ham-handed, ended up in other backwaters, she supposed, with gout and dropsy and high blood pressure. She felt, like Harry, that he was not the type. He was certainly ill-matched to his present task of managing the intractable, and even dangerous, tangle of cane.

"When is your birthday, Harry?" she asked, for she was interested in astrology and quite surprised at how many Cancer subjects came her way.

"April the twenty-first. Why?"

"Taurus the Bull," she said.

He began to bristle indignantly, then remembered his purpose and bent his head humbly, a poor, broken bull with a lance in his neck. "You mean," some instinct led him to say, "I'm like a bull in a china shop?"

Her contrition was a miracle. He listened to her hurried explanations with a glow in his heart.

"I only thought you meant I was clumsy about the place," he said. "I don't seem to cotton on to half what the others say, and I keep spilling my dinner."

"But Harry—"

"I've had my sight longer than them, and it takes more getting used to doing without it," he went on, and might have been inspired. "When you've been lucky to have your eyes so long as me, it takes some settling to." *You've still got yours* hung in the air. He managed to insinuate the idea and seem innocent of the thought, but he had lost his innocence and was as cagey as a child. His late wife would have said, "All right, you can come off it now, Harry."

Matron said, "We only want to make you happy, you know. Though sometimes you're such an old reprobate!"

After that he had to endure the impatience of being coaxed to do what he desired, and coquetry was not in his line. He became unsure of himself and the trend of the conversation, and with a Cockney adroitness let the idea of the fair simmer in Matron's mind undisturbed.

Busy again with his basketwork, he let one of the osiers snap back and hit him across the face.

"I'm no spoilsport, Harry," she said.

This daunted him; in all his life he had found that sport was spoiled by those who claimed this to be their last intention. He awaited all the other phrases—"I should hate to be a wet blanket" and "Goodness knows I don't want to criticize."

In his agitation he took up the picking knife to cut an end of cane and cut into the pad of his thumb. At first he felt no pain, but the neatness with which the blade divided his flesh alarmed him. He missed his sight when he needed to feel pain. Blood crawling between his thumb and finger put him into a panic. He imagined the bone laid bare, and his head swam. Pain coming through slowly reassured him more than Matron could.

For the rest of the evening he sat alone in his corner by the radiator, and the steady throbbing of his bandaged thumb kept him company, mixed as it was in his mind—and, no doubt, in Matron's mind too—with the promise of the fair. "I should insist on their bringing you back," she had said. "There's the rough element to contend with on a Saturday night." In other years he had been—proudly—a large part of the rough element himself.

After supper, reminded by the distant sounds of the carrousels, Miss Arbuthnot too began to discuss the rough element—which in her experience was exaggerated beyond anything Harry had ever known. Spinsterlike, she described a teeming, Hogarthian scene of pickpockets, drunkards, and what she called, contradictorily, "undesirable women." "Oh, once, I daresay, these fairs were very picturesque—the maypoles and the morris dancing. And so vividly I remember the colourful peasants I saw at the fair at Nijni Novgorod. Such beautiful embroidery. But now what is there left of such a life? So drearily commercial, as all our pleasures are."

She drove their inclinations into the corral; now no one cared to go to the fair except Harry, worldly-wise, crouched over his radiator, nursing his poor hand with his own inner vision still intact.

In the Home there was an aristocracy—never, from decency, mentioned—of those who had once, and even perhaps recently, seen, over those blind from birth. The aristocracy claimed no more than the privilege of kindness and of tact, and the feeling of superiority was tempered by the deftness and efficiency of those who had had longest to adapt themselves to being without sight. Miss Arbuthnot—blinded, Harry imagined, by her own needlework—was the eyes of them all, for she had great inventiveness and authority and could touch up a scene with the skill of an artist. Harry, finding her vision of the fair, the races, the saloon bar unacceptable, had nothing of his own to take its place—only the pig-headed reiteration, "It isn't like that."

"I used to like a roundabout when I was a girl," Mrs. Hussey said timidly.

"Well, there you have it!" said Miss Arbuthnot. "All we have salvaged of the picturesque. The last of a traditional art, in fact. For instance, the carved horses with their bright designs."

"It was going round I liked," Mrs. Hussey said.

With a tug, as of a flag unfurling, an old memory spread out across Harry's mind. He recalled himself as a boy, coming home from school with one of his friends, along the banks of a canal. It was growing dark. His child's eyes had recorded the scene, which his busy life had overlaid and preserved. Now, unexpectedly laid bare, it was more vivid than anything he had witnessed since. Sensually he evoked the magic of that time of day, with the earth about to heel over into darkness; the canal steaming faintly; cranes at a menacing angle across the sky. He and the other boy walked in single file on the muddy path, which was hoof-printed by barge horses. The tufted grass on each side was untidy and hoary with moisture; reeds, at the water's edge, lisped together. Now, in his mind, he followed this path with a painful intensity, fearing an interruption. Almost slyly he tracked down the boy he had been, who, exposed like a lens, had unconsciously taken the imprint of the moment and the place. Now, outside the scene, as if a third person, he walked behind the boys along the path; saw one, then the other, stoop and pick up a stone and skim it across the water. Without speaking, they climbed on the stacks of planks when they came to a timberyard. The air seemed to brace itself against distant thunder. The canal's surface wrinkled in a sudden breeze; then drops of rain spread rings upon it. The boys, trying the door of a long shed, found it unlocked and crept inside to shelter, wiping their wet hands down their trousers. Rain drove against the windows in a flurry, and the thunder came nearer. They stood close to each other just inside the door. The shapes which filled the shed, set out so neatly in rows, became recognizable after a while as carrousel horses, newly carved and as yet unpainted. Harry moved amongst them, ran his hand down their smooth backs, and breathed the smell of the wood. They were drawn up in ranks, pale and strange horses, awaiting their trappings and decorations and flowing tails.

The two boys spoke softly to each other, their voices muted —for the wood shavings and the sawdust, which lay everywhere like snow, had a muffling effect. Nervousness filled them. Harry forced himself to stare at the horses as if to hypnotize them, to check their rearing and bearing down, and became convinced of their hostility. Moving his eyes watchfully, he was always just too late to see a nostril quiver or a head turn, though feeling that this had happened.

The rain fell into the timberyard as if the sky had collapsed—drumming upon the roof of the shed and hissing into the canal. It was dark now, and they thought of their homes. When the horses were swallowed by shadows, the boys were too afraid to speak and strained their ears for the sound of a movement. Lightning broke across the shed, and the creatures seemed to rear up from the darkness, and all their eyes flashed glassily.

The boys, pelting along the footpath, slipping in the squelching mud, their hair in a wet fringe plastered to their foreheads, began after a while to feel their fear recede. The canal was covered with bubbles, sucked at the banks, and swirled into ratholes. Beyond the allotments was the first street lamp, and the boys leaned against it to take deep breaths and to wipe the rain from their faces. "That was only their glass eyes," Harry had said; and there, under the street lamp, the memory ended. He could not pursue himself home but was obliged to take leave of his boyhood there— the child holding his wet jacket across his chest. The evening was lying vaguely before him, with perhaps a box on the ears from Lottie Throstle for getting his boots wet—or had she fetched the tin bath in from the wall in the yard and let him soak his feet in mustard water? She had had her moods, and they defeated his memory.

Miss Arbuthnot was still talking of traditional art and craftsmanship and, rather to her vexation, was upheld in her views by the piano tuner.

Harry leaned sleepily against the radiator, tired from the mental strain of recollection—that patient stalking of his boyhood, tiring to one who had never dwelt on the past or reconsidered a scene. The intensity of the experience was so new to him that he was dazed by it, enriched, and awed by the idea of more treasure lying idle and at his disposal.

That night the pain eased him by giving a different focus to his distress. Nursing his throbbing hand to his chest, he slept his first deep and unbroken sleep since his sister's death.

On Saturday, as it grew dark, he waited for the bus at the top of the drive. His bowler hat was tilted forward, as if to match his feeling of jaunty anticipation; his scarf was tucked into his coat. Muffled up, stooping, with his head thrust from side to side, his reddened, screwed-up eyes turned upward, he looked like a great tortoise balancing on its hind legs—and burdened by the extra carapace of blindness.

At tea he had excited envy in some of the inmates when he at last overcame superstition enough to mention the fair. Miss Arbuthnot had doubled her scorn, but felt herself up against curiosity and surprise and the beginning of a reassessment, in most of their minds, of Harry's character. He had left behind a little stir of conjecture.

He heard the bus coming down the lane and stood ready, his stick raised, to hail it. The unseen headlights spread out, silhouetting him.

"You been hurting your hand?" the conductress asked, helping him into a seat.

"I just cut it. Is that old Fred up in front?"

"No, that's Evan. Fred's been on a different route, but he said to tell you he'd be waiting for you at the depot, along with Jock and Charlie."

Fred's heart sank when he saw Harry climbing down from the bus and smiling like a child. Saddling his friends with the old geezer for an evening was too much of a responsibility, and constraint and false heartiness marked the beginning of the outing. He had explained and apologized over and over again for the impulse which had brought Harry into the party. "Why, that's all right, Fred," they had assured him.

He thought that a beer or two at the Wheatsheaf would make them feel better, but after so much enforced abstinence the drink went to Harry's head with swift effect. He became boastful, swaggering. He invited laughter and threw in a few coarse jests for good measure. Sitting by the fire, his coat trailing about him, he looked a shocking old character, Fred thought. The beer dripped onto his knees; above the straining fly buttons his waistcoat bulged, looped with the tarnished chain of a watch he kept winding and holding to his ear, although he could no longer read it. Every so often he knocked his bowler hat straight with his stick—a slick music-hall gesture. Cocky and garrulous, he attracted attention from those not yet tired of his behaviour or responsible for it, as Fred was. They offered cigarettes and more drink.

When at last he was persuaded to go, he lurched into a table, slopping beer from glasses.

Down the wide main street the fair booths were set out. Their lights spread upward through the yellowing leaves of the trees. The tunes of competing carrousels engulfed Harry in a confusion of sound. The four men stopped at a stall for a plateful of whelks and were joined by another bus driver and his wife, whose shrill peacock laughter flew out above all the other sounds.

"How are you keeping, Harry?" she asked. She was eating some pink candy floss on a stick, and her lips and the inside of her mouth were crimson from it. Harry could smell the sickly raspberry smell of her breath.

"Quite nicely, thanks. I had a bit of a cold, but I can't complain."

"Ever such a lot of colds about," she said vaguely.

"And lately I seem to be troubled with my hearing." He could not forgo this chance to talk of himself.

"Well, never mind. Can't have it all ways, I suppose."

He doesn't have it many ways, Fred thought.

"You ought to take me through the Haunted House, you know, Harry. I can't get anyone else to."

"You don't want to go along with an old codger like me."

"I wouldn't trust him in the dark, Vi," Fred said.

"I'll risk it."

She sensed his apprehension as they turned towards the sideshow. From behind the canvas façade, with its painted skeletons, came the sound of wheels running on a track, and spasms of wild laughter. Harry tripped over a cable, and she took his arm. "You're a real old sport," she told him. She paid at the entrance and helped him into a little car like a toast rack. They sat close together. She finished her candy, threw away the stick, and began to lick her fingers. "I've got good care of you," she said. "It's only a bit of kids' fun."

The car started forward, jolting at sharp bends, where sheeted ghosts leaned over them and luminous skulls shone in the darkness. Vi outlaughed everyone, screaming into Harry's ear and gripping his arm with both hands.

"It isn't much for *you,*" she kept saying sympathetically. He couldn't see any of the horrific sights that made her gasp, but the jerking, the swift running on, the narrow (he guessed) avoidance of unseen obstacles made him tremble. The close smell was frightening, and when, as part of the macabre adventure, synthetic cobwebs trailed over his face and bony fingers touched his shoulder, he ducked his head fearfully.

"Well, you *are* an old baby," Vi said.

They came out into the light and the crowds again, and as they went towards her husband and the others, she put up her raspberry lips and kissed his cheek.

Her behaviour troubled him. She seemed to rehearse flirtatiousness with him for its own sake—unless it were to excite her audience. She expected no consequence from her coquetry, as if his blindness had made him less than a man. Her husband rarely spoke, and never to her, and Harry could not see his indifferent look.

With ostentatious care Vi guided him through the crowds, her arm in his so closely that he could feel her bosom against his elbow. He was tired now—physically, and with the strain of being at everybody's mercy and of trying to take his colour from other people. His senses, with their extra burden, were fatigued. The braying music cuffed his ears until he longed to clap his hands over them. His uncertain stumblings had made his step drag. Drifting smells—shellfish, petrol, and Vi's raspberry breath—began to nauseate him.

At the coconut shy she was shriller than ever. She stood inside the net, over the ladies' line, and screamed each time she missed, and, when a coconut rocked and did not fall, accused the proprietor, in piteous baby talk, of trickery.

Her husband had walked on, yawning, heedless of her importunities—for she *had* to have a coconut, just as she had *had* to have her fortune told and her turn on the swing boats.

Jock and Charlie followed, and they were lost in the crowd. Fred stayed and watched Vi's anger growing. When he knocked down a coconut she claimed it at once as a trophy. She liked to leave a fair laden with such tributes to her sexual prowess.

"Well, it's just too bad," Fred said, "because I'm taking it home to my wife."

"You're mean. Isn't he mean, Harry?"

Fred, coming closer to her, said softly as he held the coconut to his ear and rattled the milk, "You can have it on one condition."

"What's that?"

"You guess," he said.

She turned her head quickly. "Harry, you'll get a coconut for me, won't you?" She ran her hands up under the lapels of Harry's coat in a film-actressy way and rearranged his scarf.

"That's right, Harry," Fred said. "You told me the other day you were going to have a try. You can't do worse than

Vi." Her fury relaxed him. He threw the coconut from one hand to the other and whistled softly, watching her.

Harry was aware that he was being put to some use, but the childish smile he had worn all the evening did not change; it expressed anxiety and the desire to please. Only by pleasing could he live. By complying—as clown, as eunuch—he earned the scraps and shreds they threw to him, the odds and ends left over from their everyday life.

Fred and Vi filled his arms with the wooden balls and led him to the front of the booth. Vi took his stick and stepped back. Someone behind her whispered, "He's blind. How dreadful!" and she turned and said, "Real spry old character, isn't he?" in a proprietary voice. More people pressed up to watch, murmuring sympathetically.

"Aim straight ahead," Fred was saying, and the man in charge was adding his advice. Harry's smile wrinkled up his face and his scarred-looking eyes. "How's that?" he cried, flinging his arm up violently and throwing. The crowd encouraged him, anxious that he should be successful. He threw again.

Fred stepped back, close to Vi, who avoided his glance. Staring ahead, still whistling, he put his hand out and gripped her wrist. She turned her arm furiously, but no one noticed.

"You've been asking for something all the evening, haven't you?" he asked her in a light conversational tone. "One of these days you're going to get it, see? That's right, Harry!" he shouted. "That was a near one! Proper old character. You can't help admiring him."

Vi's hand was still. She looked coolly in front of her, but Fred could sense a change of pulse, an excitement in her, and almost nodded to himself when she began to twist her fingers in his, with a vicious lasciviousness he had foreseen.

A cheer went up as Harry's throw went near to his target. "Next round on the house," the owner said. Harry's smile changed to a desperate grin. His bowler hat was crooked, and all his movements were impeded by his heavy overcoat. Noise shifted and roared round him until he felt giddy and began to sweat.

Insanely the carrousel horses rose and plunged, as if spurred on by the music and the lateness of the hour. Sparks spluttered from the electric cars. Above the trees the sky was bruised with a reddish stain, a polluted light, like a miasma given off by the fair.

The rough good will of the crowd went to Harry's head, and he began to clown and boast, as if he were drunk. Fred and Vi seemed to have vanished. Their voices were lost. He could hear only the carrousel and the thud of the wooden balls as he threw them against the canvas screen, and he feared the moment when his act was over and he must turn, empty-handed, hoping to be claimed.

"Taking Mother Out"

"Give the credit where it is due," Mrs. Crouch said, smiling at her son.

We had, of course, been marvelling at her youthfulness. Every gesture she made, even the most simple, seemed calculated to defy old age. She constantly drew our attention to her eighty years, referred to herself as an old fogy, insisted on this when we were obliged to demur. And then insisted on insisting. We offered her a drink. She became husky, Marie Lloydish, a little *broad*. Her glass of gin she turned into a music-hall act. A further little speech was made over a cigarette, my brother waiting with his lighter flaring ready while she launched off into an explanation about herself—how she liked a bit of fun, liked young people, was as old as she felt, merely.

I glanced at her son, but not as if he were anything within my or anybody's reach. He was flashy, cynical, one of those men who knows about everything; makes sinister implications of rumours in the City, panic in the Cabinet; hints at inside information; has seen everything, seen through everything; known everybody, loved nobody; bought everything at a special price, and sold it again at a great profit. His mother admired him of all her children the most. She displayed him, was indebted to him, gave credit to him, as she was doing now.

He looked in her direction and smiled, a little bored with the elderly bird-watcher who had sat down beside him to describe without pause his day on the marshes. He was right to be bored by the bird-watcher—a relation of ours who menaced our every summer.

The evening light enhances those marshes. We sipped our drinks, narrowed our eyes, gazing down over the green flatness where masts in the middle of a field seemed to indicate the estuary. Little silences fell over us from time to time. The gentle vista before us, the gradual cadences, the close-cropped grass tufted with rough weeds which the slow-moving sheep had left, untidy little sheets of water, far off the glitter of the sea—all of this held our attention, even from one another, for English people love a view. Only the bird-watcher droned on.

Mrs. Crouch twirled her glass, brushed at her skirt, examined her rings, wondering, I guessed, what the spotted crake had to do with her and how wonderfully she carried her age. She decided to begin a counter-conversation and turned to my brother, raising her voice, for she was a little deaf and usually shouted.

"I hope, my dear, you won't think I tie Roy to my apron strings. As a matter of fact, I am always saying to him, 'Roy,' I say, 'you ought to be taking out a beautiful young blonde instead of your old mother.' But he won't have it. Of course I love my little outings, going out and meeting young people. When I'm asked how it is I carry my age so well, I say it's being with young people, and most of all being with Roy. He won't *let* me settle down. 'Come along, Mother,' he says, 'let's go off on a binge.' " She savoured this word, chuckling. My brother fidgeted gloomily with his wristwatch. Roy Crouch fidgeted with his too.

"No," said the bird-watcher, as if contradicting himself, "not a common sight, but a remarkable one, the male bird sitting on the nest. No mistaking that, even at a distance, through fieldglasses. The female is smaller and duller."

"Quite," said Roy nastily.

"I've had a full life," his mother was saying. My brother swallowed and glanced out across the salt marshes.

"Did you ever see a Richard's pipit?" Roy suddenly asked.

"No," said the bird-watcher shortly. "Did you?"

"Yes."

The bird-watcher turned right round in his chair and stared at him. He could not call him a liar, but he said, "Then you were very fortunate, sir. May I inquire where?"

"In Norfolk," Roy said carelessly.

"Very fortunate," the bird-watcher repeated, still glaring.

"I think that's why Roy likes to take me out, because I enjoy myself."

"I expect so," my brother agreed.

I refilled glasses. The bird-watcher recovered. He began to talk of the water-rail, how he had lain in a bed of reeds and counted seven pairs that morning. A wonderful sight. Perhaps not Richard's pipits, you bounder, he seemed to imply —but a wonderful sight all the same.

"Talking of wonderful sights," said Roy, getting into his stride, "I was staying near the Severn Estuary in the spring and saw a very unusual thing—rather a romantic sight." He laughed apologetically. "I happened to look out of my bedroom window one night when it was quite dark, and I could see something moving down in the water-meadows, something rippling." He rippled his fingers, to show us. "Something that shimmered." His hand shimmered. "I stood very still and watched, hardly able to believe my eyes, but at last I realized what it was." He looked at the bird-watcher and at me. My brother was out of this conversation.

"But I really don't think," Mrs. Crouch was telling him, "that the new tunes are half so jolly as the old . . ."

"And what do you think it was?" Roy asked us.

We did not know.

We did not know, we said.

"Eels," he said impressively, "young eels—or rather, I should say elvers," he corrected himself. "I shall never forget that sight. It was ghostly, unreal. In a silver flood they rippled through the grass in the moonlight, through a little stream and then on up the slope—beautiful. They come up from the sea, you know. Every spring. I've heard people say they *couldn't* travel across land, but there it was. I saw with my own eyes."

My brother was nearly asleep. Mrs. Crouch said suddenly, testily, "What are you all nodding your heads so solemnly about?"

"Eels," I said lightly.

"Eels? Oh, eels! Why, only last night some friends of ours, a Mr. and Mrs. Sibley, were telling us about an experience they had when they were staying near the Severn Estuary. They were going to bed one night and Mr. Sibley happened to look out of the window, and he suddenly called out to Mrs. Sibley, 'Just come and look at this,' he said. 'There's something moving down there on the grass,' and Mrs. Sibley said, 'Frank, do you know what I think those are? I do believe they're eels, young eels'—I forget the name she gave to them. What was that word, Roy?"

"No one has a drink," I cried, running frantically from one glass to another. The bird-watcher looked gravely, peacefully at the view.

"Thank you, dear," said Mrs. Crouch. "I am not at all sure that I haven't had too much already. What *was* that word, Roy? I have it at the tip of my tongue."

"Elvers," he muttered and took a great swallow at his gin. He looked dejected, worn, as old as his mother almost. They might have been husband and wife.

A Sad Garden

The wall running round the small garden was pitted with hundreds of holes, and rusty nails flying little rags were to be seen in the spaces between the espaliers—the branches like candelabra, the glossy leaves, the long rough brown pears, the thin-skinned yellow ones and the mottled ones which lay against the bricks.

"There is no one to eat the fruit," said Sybil. "Take what you want." She handed her sister-in-law a small ripe William and sauntered away down the garden.

"Well, I certainly will," said Kathy, following eagerly after. "I could do with some for bottling."

"Take them, then. Take them." Sybil sat down on a stone seat at the end of the path. The day was nearly gone, but the brick wall still gave out its warmth. "Mind the wasps, Audrey," she said. "They're getting sleepy." (Audrey! she thought, watching her little niece coming carefully up the path. What a stupid name!)

The garden was filled with the smell of rotting fruit. Pears lay about on the paths, and wasps tunnelled into their ripeness. Audrey stepped timidly over them. She was all white and clean—face, serge coat, and socks. Her mother held the William pear in her gloved hand. "You shall have it when we get home," she promised. "Not in that coat, dear."

Sybil sighed sharply.

"Well, if you really mean it, I could slip back home for the big garden basket," Kathy went on. She was doubtful always and nervous with her sister-in-law.

The others had long ago given up calling on Sybil. "She's had trouble," they admitted. "We can grant her that. But she makes no effort."

Kathy was the only one who was too kindhearted to give in. Every week she called. "You see, she's all on her own," she would tell the others. "We've got one another, but she's lost everything—husband and son. I try to think what that would mean to me." (Not that she had a son; but she had Audrey.)

"She was like it before," they reminded her. "Before ever Ralph died. Or Adam. Always queer, always moody and lazy and rude. She thinks she's too clever for us. After all, it's safer to be ordinary."

Kathy would try to explain, excuse, forgive, and they would never listen to her, for it was instinct that guided them, not reason. "She led Ralph the hell of a dance, anyway," they would always conclude.

Kathy glanced at Sybil now, sitting there on the stone seat, leaning back against the wall, with her eyes half closed and a suggestion about her of power ill concealed, of sarcasm, of immunity from human contact. Kathy—the others said she was deficient in instinct—saw nothing she could dislike—merely a tired woman who was lonely. There was nothing against her except that she had once been brave when she should have been overcome, and had spoken of her only child with too much indifference—and as for leading Ralph a dance, she had merely laughed at him sometimes and admired him, it seemed, somewhat less than they had always done at home.

"Well, fetch your basket," she was saying.

Kathy hesitated. "Coming, Audrey?"

"Oh, she can stay," said Sybil.

"Well, mind your socks; then they'll be clean for school tomorrow. I'll be back in a minute or two. Be a good girl."

Audrey had no idea of being anything else. She sat down timidly on the edge of the seat and watched her mother disappear round the side of the house.

Sybil looked at her without enthusiasm. "Do you like school?" she asked suddenly, harshly.

"Yes, thank you, Auntie."

Sybil's fingers wandered over the seat as if from habit until the tops of them lay at last in the rough grooves of some carved initials—the letters A. K. R. She had smacked him for that, for always cutting his name into other people's property, had taken away his chisel. When she did that he had stared at her in hatred—wild, beautiful, a stain on his mouth from the blackberries or some purple fruit, and a stain of anger on his cheeks. Her fingers gripped the seat.

"So you like school and never play truant?"

"Oh, no, Auntie"—a little shocked giggle. The child swung her feet, looking down placidly at her clean socks.

Thank God I never had a daughter, thought Sybil. "Would you like some fruit?"

"Mummy said not to in this coat."

"What *would* you like?" Sybil asked in exasperation, thrusting her hair back with a gesture of impatience.

The child looked puzzled.

"A swing? Would you like a swing?"

Audrey's mouth shaped a "No," but, seeing her aunt's look, she changed her mind and smiled and nodded, feigning delight.

She sat down on the swing and put her shiny shoes primly together. Even the seat of the swing was carved with initials. She knew that they were her cousin's and that he was dead, that it had been his swing; she remembered him refusing to allow her to sit on it. She did so now with pleasurable guilt, looking primly round at the clumps of Michaelmas daisies as if she half expected him to come bursting from them in anger. She allowed herself to rock gently to and fro.

Aunt Sybil stopped on her way to the house. "Can't you go higher than that?" she said, and she took the seat in two hands, drew it back to her, and then thrust it far away so that Audrey went high up into the leaves and fruit. Birds rose off the top of the tree in a panic.

"That's how Adam used to go," Sybil shouted as Audrey flew down again. "Right up into the leaves. He used to kick the pears down with his feet."

"I don't—I don't—" cried Audrey.

As she flew down, Sybil put her hands in the small of the child's back and thrust her away again. "Higher, higher," Adam used to shout. He was full of wickedness and devilry. She went on pushing, without thinking of Audrey. The garden was darkening. A question mark of white smoke rose from the quenched bonfire beside the rubbish heap.

"There you go. There you go," she cried. And she thought: But what a boring little girl—"Yes, Mummy. No, thank you, Auntie." I'd never have Adam tied to my apron strings. I'd push him out into the world. Push him. She gave a vehemence to her thought, and Audrey, with her hair streaming among the branches, flew dizzily away. Frantically now her aunt pushed her, crying, "There you go. There you go."

The child, whiter than ever, was unable to speak, to cry out. She sensed something terribly wrong and yet something which was inevitable and not surprising. Each time she dropped to earth a wave of darkness hit her face, and then she would fly up again in a wild agony. A strand of hair caught in some twigs and was torn from her head.

Sybil stood squarely on the grass. As the swing came down she put up her hands and, with the tips of her fingers and yet with all her strength, she pushed. She had lost consciousness and control and cried out each time exultingly, "There you go. There you go"—until all her body was trembling.

Kathy came screaming up the path.

Oasis of Gaiety

After luncheon Dosie took off her shoes and danced all round the room. Her feet were plump and arched, and the varnish on her toenails shone through her stockings.

Her mother was sitting on the floor, playing roulette with some of her friends. She was always called "Auntie" except by Dosie, who "darling-ed" her in the tetchy manner of one of two women living in the same house, and by her son, Thomas, who stolidly said "Mother"—a démodé word, Auntie felt, half insulting.

On Sunday afternoons most of Auntie's set returned to their families when the midday champagne was finished. They scattered to the other houses round the golf course, to doze on loggias, snap at their children, and wonder where their gaiety had fled. Only Mrs. Wilson—who was a widow and dreaded her empty house—Ricky Jimpson, and the goatish Fergy Burns stayed on. More intimate than a member of the family, more inside than a friend, Fergy supported Auntie's idea of herself better than anyone else did, and, at times and in ways that he knew she couldn't mind, he sided with Dosie and Thomas against her.

In some of the less remote parts of Surrey, where the nineteen-twenties are perpetuated, such pockets of stale and elderly gaiety remain. They are blank as the surrounding landscape of fir trees and tarnished water.

Sunshine, especially blinding to the players after so much champagne, slanted into the room, which looked preserved, sealed off. Pinkish-grey cretonnes, ruched cushions with tassels, piles of gramophone records, and a velvet Maurice Chevalier doll recalled the stage-sets of those forgotten comedies about weekends in the country and domestic imbroglios.

Auntie's marmoset sat on the arm of a chair, looking down sadly at the players and eating grapes, which he peeled with delicate, worn fingers and sharp teeth. His name was Rizzio. Auntie loved to name her possessions—everything: her car (called the Bitch, a favourite word of her youth), her fur coat, the rather noisy cistern in the w.c. Even some of her old cardigans and shawls had nicknames and personalities. Her friends seemed not to find this tiresome. They played the game strenuously and sometimes sent Christmas presents to the inanimate objects. In exchange for all the fun and champagne they were required only to assist the fantasy and preserve the past. Auntie thought of herself as a sport and a scream. (No one knew how her nickname had originated, for neither niece nor nephew had ever appeared to substantiate it.) "I did have a lovely hey-day," she would say in her husky voice. "Girls of Dosie's age have never had anything." But Dosie had had two husbands already, not to count the incidentals, as Thomas said.

Thomas was her much younger brother, something of

an incidental flowering himself. "Auntie's last bit of nonsense," people called him. Fifteen years and their different worlds separated brother and sister. He was of a more serious generation and seemed curiously practical, disabused, unemotional. His military service was a life beyond their imagination. They (pitying him, though recoiling from him) vaguely envisaged hutted sites at Aldershot and boorish figures at football on muddy playing fields with mists rising. Occasionally, at weekends, he arrived, wearing sour-smelling khaki, which seemed to rub almost raw his neck and wrists. He would clump into the pub in his great Army boots and drink mild-and-bitter at his mother's expense, cagey about laying down a halfpenny of his own.

He made Fergy feel uneasy. Fergy had, Auntie often said, an impossible conscience. Watching bullocks being driven into a slaughterhouse had once taken him off steak for a month, and now, when he saw Thomas in khaki, he could only remember his own undergraduate days—gilded youth, fun with fireworks and chamber pots, debutantes arriving in May Week, driving his red M.G. to the Beetle and Wedge for the Sunday-morning session. But Thomas had no M.G. He had only the 7:26 back to Aldershot. If he ever had any gaiety his mother did not discover it; if he had any friends he did not bring them forward. Auntie was, Fergy thought, a little mean with him, a little on the tight side. She used endearments to him, but as if in utter consternation. He was an uncouth cuckoo in her nest. His hands made excruciating sounds on the silk cushions. Often in bars she would slip him a pound to pay his way, yet here he was this afternoon, making as neat and secret a little pile as one would wish to see.

He played with florins, doubling them slowly, giving change where required, tucking notes into the breast pocket of his battle dress, carefully buttoning them away as if no one was to be trusted. He had a rather breathy concentration, as he had had as a child, crouching over snakes-and-ladders; his hands, scooping up the coins, looked, Auntie thought, like great paws.

Only Mrs. Wilson's concentration could match his, but she had none of his stealthy deliberation. She had lost a packet, she proclaimed, but no one listened. She kept putting her hand in her bag and raking about, bringing out only a handkerchief, with which she touched the corners of her mouth. The others seemed to her quite indifferent to the fortunes of the game—Fergy, for instance, who was the banker, pushing Thomas's winnings across to him with no change of expression and no hesitation in his flow of talk.

Auntie gave a tiny glance of dislike at her son as he slipped some coins into his pocket. She could imagine him counting them all up, going back in the train. In her annoyance she added a brutish look to his face. She sighed, but it was almost imperceptible and quite unperceived, the slightest intake of breath, as she glanced round at her friends, the darlings, who preserved her world—drinking her whisky, switching the radio away from the news to something gayer, and fortifying her against the dreary postwar world her son so typified. Mrs. Wilson also was a little dreary. Although trying gallantly, she had no real aptitude for recklessness and easily became drunk, when she would talk about her late husband and what a nice home they had had.

"Oh, Dosie, do sit down!" Auntie said.

Dosie was another who could not drink. She would become gayer and gayer and more and more taunting to poor Ricky Jimpson. Now she was dancing on his winnings. He smiled wanly. After the game he would happily give her the lot, but while he was playing it was sacred.

What Dosie herself gave for all she had from him was something to conjecture. Speculation, beginning with the obviously shameful, had latterly run into a maze of contradictions. Perhaps—and this was even more derogatory—she *did* only bestow taunts and abuse. She behaved like a very wilful child, as if to underline the fact that Ricky was old enough to be her father. Rather grey-faced (he had, he thought, a duodenal ulcer, and the vast quantity of whisky he drank was agony to him), he would sit and smile at her naughty ways, and sometimes when she clapped her hands, as if she pretended he was her slave, he would show that this was not pretence but very truth, and hurry to carry out her wishes.

Dosie, with one hand on the piano to steady herself, went through some of the *barre* exercises she had learned as a child at ballet class. Her joints snapped and crackled with a sound like a fire kindling.

"You are a deadly lot," she suddenly said and yawned out at the garden. "Put ten shillings on *rouge* for me, Ricky. I always win if you do it."

At least she doesn't lose if it isn't her money, Mrs. Wilson thought, wondering if she could ever, in a rallying way, make such a request of Fergy.

The hot afternoon, following the champagne, made them all drowsy. Only Ricky Jimpson sat up trimly. Fergy, looking at Mrs. Wilson's bosom, which her décolleté blouse too generously tendered, thought that in no time it would be all she had to offer. He imagined her placing it on, perhaps, *zéro*—her last gesture.

Quite frightful, Auntie thought, the way Thomas's brow furrowed because he had lost two shillings. He was transparently sulky, like a little boy. All those baked beans in canteens made him stodgy and impossible. She hadn't visualized having such a son, or such a world for him to live in.

"We can really do nothing for young people," she had once told Mrs. Wilson. "Nothing, nowadays, but try to preserve for them some of the old days, keep up our standards, and give them an inkling of what things used to be, make a little oasis of gaiety for them." That had been during what she called "the late war." Thomas was home from school for the Christmas holidays. With tarnished prewar tinsel Auntie was decorating the Christmas tree, though to this, as to most things, Thomas was quite indifferent. He had spent the holidays bicycling slowly round and round the lawn on the white, rimed grass. In the evenings, when his mother's friends came for drinks, he collected his books and went noticeably to his room. The books, on mathematics, were dull but mercifully concerned with things as they were, and this he preferred to all the talk about the tarnished prewar days. He could not feel that the present day was any of his doing. For the grown-ups to scorn what they had bequeathed to him seemed tactless. He ignored those conversations until his face looked mulish and immune. His mother arranged for his adenoids to be removed, but he continued to be closed up and unresponsive.

Dosie was so different; she might almost be called a ringleader. She made her mother feel younger than ever—

"really more like a sister," Auntie said, showing that this was a joke by saying it with a Cockney accent. Oh, Dosie was the liveliest girl, except that sometimes she went too far. The oasis of gaiety her mother provided became obviously too small, and she was inclined then to go off into the desert and cry havoc. But Auntie thought her daughter mischievous, not desperate.

"Either play or not," she told her sharply, for sometimes the girl irritated her.

But Dosie, at the french windows, took no notice. She could feel the sun striking through her thin frock, and she seemed to unfold in the warmth, like a flower. In the borders lilies stood to attention in the shimmering air, their petals glazed and dusty with pollen. The scent was wonderful.

"I shall bathe in the pool," she said over her shoulder. The pool—a long rectangle of water thick with plants—was deep, and Dosie had never learned to swim, had always floundered wildly.

Only Ricky Jimpson remonstrated.

"She can't swim," Auntie said, dismissing her daughter's nonsense. "Does anyone *want* to go on playing?"

Mrs. Wilson certainly did not. She had never believed in last desperate flings, throwing good money after bad. In games of chance there was no certainty but that she would lose; even the law of averages worked against her. What she wanted now was a cup of tea and aspirins, for champagne agreed with her no better than roulette. She felt lost. Her widowhood undermined her, and she no longer felt loved.

But who was loved—in this room, for instance? Mrs. Wilson often thought that her husband would not have dared to die if he had known she would drift into such company. "What *you* need, darling, is a nice, cosy woman friend," Fergy had said years ago when she had reacted in bewilderment to his automatic embrace. He had relinquished her at once in a weary, bored way, and ignored her coldly ever since. His heartless perception frightened her. Despite her acceptance of—even clinging to—their kind of life, and her acquiescence in every madness, every racket, she had not disguised from him that what she wanted was her dull, good husband back and a nice evening with the wireless; perhaps, too, a middle-aged woman friend to go shopping with, to talk about slimming and recipes. Auntie never discussed those things. She was the kind of woman men liked. She amused them with her scatterbrained chatter and innuendo and the fantasy she wove, the stories she told, about herself. When she was with women she rested. Mrs. Wilson could not imagine her feeling unsafe, or panicking when the house emptied. She seemed self-reliant and efficient. She and Dosie sometimes quarrelled, or appeared to be quarrelling, with lots of "But, *darling!*" and "*Must* you be such a fool, sweetie?" Yet only Thomas, the symbol of the postwar world, was really an affront. Him she could not assimilate. He was the grit that nothing turned into a pearl—neither gaiety nor champagne. He remained blank, impervious. He took his life quite seriously, made no jokes about the Army, was silent when his mother said, "Oh, *why go?* Catch the last train or wait until morning. In fact, why don't you desert? Dosie and I could hide you in the attic. It would be the greatest fun. Or be ill. Get some awful soldier's disease."

Dosie was blocking the sunlight from the room, and Mrs.

Wilson suddenly felt gooseflesh on her arms and cramp in her legs from sitting on the floor.

Ricky Jimpson put his winnings in his pocket without a glance at them. He sat, bent slightly forward, with one hand pressed to his waist. He smiled brilliantly if he caught anybody's eye, but his face soon reassembled itself to its look of static melancholy. The smile was an abrupt disorganization. His eyes rarely followed Dosie. He seemed rather to be listening to her, even when she was silent. He was conscious of her in some other way than visually. His spirit *attended* to her, caught up in pain though he was.

The roulette cloth was folded and put away. The marmoset was busy tearing one of the cushion tassels. Then, to Mrs. Wilson's relief, the door opened and a maid pushed in a trolley with a jazzy black and orange pottery tea set and some rolled-up bread and butter.

Dosie wandered out across the gravelled path in her stocking feet. The garden, the golf course beyond it, and all the other wisteria-covered, balconied Edwardian villas at its perimeter seemed to slant and swoon in the heat. Her exasperation weakened and dispersed. She always felt herself leaving other people behind; they lagged after her recklessness. Even in making love she felt the same isolation—that she was speeding on into a country where no one would pursue her. Each kiss was an act of division. Follow me! she willed them—a succession of them, all shadowy. They could not follow, or know to what cold distances she withdrew. Her punishment for them was mischief, spite, a little gay cruelty, but nothing drastic. She had no beauty, for there was none to inherit, but she was a bold and noticeable woman.

When Fergy joined her in the garden he put his arm across her shoulders and they walked down the path towards the pool. Water lilies lay picturesquely on the green surface. The oblong of water was bordered by ornamental grasses in which dragonflies glinted. A concrete gnome was fishing at the edge.

They stood looking at the water, lulled by the heat and the beauty of the afternoon. When he slipped his arm closer round her she felt herself preparing, as of old, for flight. Waywardly she moved from him. She stripped seeds off a tall grass viciously, and scattered them on the water. Goldfish rose, then sank away dejectedly.

"Let us throw in this bloody little dwarf," Dosie said, "and you can cry for help. They will think I am drowning." She began to rock the gnome from side to side. Small brown frogs like crumpled leaves leaped away into the grass.

"Auntie dotes on the little creature," Fergy said. "She has a special nickname for him."

"So have I."

Together they lifted the gnome and threw him out towards the centre of the pool.

"I always loathed the little beast," Dosie said.

"Help!" Fergy cried. "For *God's* sake, help!"

Dosie watched the house, her face alight, her eyebrows lifted in anticipation. Rings widened and faded on the water.

Ricky Jimpson dashed through the french windows and ran towards the pool, his face whiter than ever, his hand to his side. When he saw them both standing there he stopped. His look of desperation vanished. He smiled his brilliant, dutiful smile, but, receiving one of his rare glances, Dosie saw in his eyes utter affliction, forlornness.

That evening Thomas, on his way back to Aldershot, met Syd at the top of the station subway—as per usual arrangement, Syd had said when they parted the day before. Their greeting was brief, and they went in silence towards the restaurant, shouldering their way along the crowded platform. In the bar they ordered two halves of mild-and-bitter and two pieces of pork pie.

Syd pushed back his greasy beret and scratched his head. Then he broke open the pie to examine the inside—the pink gristle and tough grey jelly.

"What they been up to this time?" he asked.

"The usual capering about. My mother was rather lit up last night and kept doing the Charleston."

"Go on!"

"But I suppose that's better than the Highland Fling," Thomas said. "Pass the mustard."

Syd, whose own mother rarely moved more than, very ponderously, from sink to gas stove, was fascinated. "Like to've seen it," he said. "From a distance."

"What did you do?" Thomas asked.

"Went to the Palais, Saturday night, along with Viv. Never got up till twelve this morning, then went round to the local. Bit of a read this afternoon, then went for a stroll along with Viv. You know, up by the allotments. Had a nice lie-down in the long grass. She put her elbow in a cow-pat. Laugh!" He threw back his head and laughed there and then.

"Same again," Thomas said to the barmaid. "Want some more pie, Syd?"

"No, ta. I had me tea."

"I made thirty-four bob," Thomas said, tapping his breast pocket.

"You can make mine a pint then," Syd said. But Thomas didn't say anything. They always drank halves. He looked at Syd and wondered what his mother would say of him. He often wondered that. But she would never have the chance. He looked quite fiercely round the ugly restaurant room, with its chromium tables, ringed and sticky, thick china, glass domes over the museum pieces of pork pie. The look of the place calmed him, as Syd's company did—something he could grasp, *his* world.

"Don't know how they stick that life, week after week," Thomas said. "My sister threw a garden ornament in the pond—pretended she'd fallen in herself. A sort of dwarf," he added vaguely.

"What for?" Syd asked.

"I think she was fed up," Thomas said, trying to understand. But he lived in two irreconcilable worlds.

Syd only said, "Rum. Could they fish it out again?"

"No one tried. We had tea then." He gave up trying to explain what he did not comprehend, and finished his beer.

"Better get a move on," Syd said, using as few consonants as possible.

"Yes, I suppose so." Thomas looked at the clock.

"The old familiar faces."

"You're right," Thomas agreed contentedly.

The Beginning of a Story

They could hear the breathing through the wall. Ronny sat watching Marian, who had her fingers in her ears as she read. Sometimes he leaned forward and reached for a log and put it on the fire, and for a second her eyes would dwell on his movements, on his young, bony wrist shot out of his sleeve, and then, like a lighthouse swinging its beam away, she would withdraw her attention and go back to her book.

A long pause in the breathing would make them glance at each other questioningly, and then, as it was hoarsely resumed, they would fall away from each other again, he to his silent building of the fire and she to her solemn reading of *Lady Audley's Secret*.

He thought of his mother, Enid, in the next room, sitting at her own mother's deathbed, and he tried to imagine her feelings, but her behaviour had been so calm all through his grandmother's illness that he could not. It is different for the older ones, he thought, for they are used to people dying. More readily he could picture his father at the pub, accepting drinks and easy sympathy. "Nothing I can do," he would be saying. "You only feel in the way." Tomorrow night, perhaps, "A happy release" would be his comfortable refrain, and solemnly, over their beer, they would all agree.

Once Marian said to Ronny, "Why don't you get something to do?"

"Such as what?"

"Oh, don't ask me. It's not my affair." These last few days Marian liked, as often as she could, to dissociate herself from the family. As soon as the grandmother became ill the other lodger, a girl from the same factory as Marian, had left. Marian had stayed on, but with her fingers stuck in her ears, or going about with a blank immunity, polite and distant to Enid. They were landlady and lodger to each other, no more, Marian constantly implied.

"Well, you could make some tea," she said at last to Ronny, feeling exasperation at his silent contemplation of her. He moved obediently and began to unhook cups from the dresser without a sound, setting them carefully in their saucers on a tray—the pink and gilt one with the moss rose for Marian, a large white one with a gold clover leaf for his mother.

"You take it in to her," he said when the tea was ready. He had a reason for asking her, wishing to test his belief that Marian was afraid to go into that other room. She guessed this and snapped her book shut.

"Lazy little swine," she said and took up his mother's cup.

Enid rose as Marian opened the door. The room was bright and warm. It was the front room, and the Sunday furniture had been moved to make space for the bed. The old woman was half sitting up, but her head was thrown back upon a heap of pillows. Her arms were stretched out over the counterpane, just as her daughter had arranged them. Her mouth, without teeth, was a grey cavern. Except for the breathing, she might have been dead.

Enid had been sitting up with her for nights, and she stood stiffly now, holding the cup of tea, her eyes dark with fatigue. I ought to offer, thought Marian, but I'd be terrified to be left alone in here.

She went back to Ronny, who looked at her now with respect added to all the other expressions on his face. His father had come back from the pub and was spreading his hairy hands over the fire to get warm. He was beery and lugubrious. They were all afraid of Enid. At any sound from the other room they flicked glances at one another.

"Poor old gel," said Ronny's father over and over again. "Might as well get to bed, Marian. No need for you to make yourself ill."

Ronny found his father's way of speaking and his look at the girl intolerable.

Marian had been waiting for someone to make the suggestion. "Well—" She hesitated. "No sense, I suppose . . ."

"That's right," said the older man.

She went out to the sink in the scullery and slipped her shoulders out of her blouse. She soaped a flannel under the icy water and passed it quickly over her throat, gathering up her hair at the back to wash her neck, curving one arm, then the other, over her head as she soaped her armpits.

Ronny and his father sat beside the fire, listening to the water splashing into the bowl. When they heard the wooden sound as Marian pulled at the roller towel, the older man glanced at the door and moved, stirred by the thought of the young girl.

It was one of the moments of hatred that the son often felt for him, but it seemed to make no impression on his father.

Marian came in, fresh, her face shiny, her blouse carelessly buttoned. "Well, good night," she said, and opened the door behind which stairs led up to the little bedrooms. "If you want me, you know where I am."

There was no sophistication in either man to see the ambiguity of her words; they simply took them to mean what she intended.

The door closed, and they heard her creak upstairs and overhead. They went on sitting by the fire, and neither spoke. Occasional faint beer smells came from the father. It did not occur to him to go into the other room to his wife. Ronny took the tea things into the scullery and washed up. It was dark out there and lit by a very small oil lamp. He remained there for as long as he thought he could without being questioned. The tap dripped into the sink. He smelled the soap she had used. He could no longer hear the breathing.

Marian lay between the rough twill sheets, shivering. Her feet were like ice, although she had rolled them in her cardigan. The only hot-water bottle was in the bed downstairs. She hated this house but had no energy to move from it. Or had she stayed because of that sickened curiosity that always forced her to linger by hearses while coffins were carried out? Ron too, she thought. It isn't right for us. We're young. In the morning I'm not fit for work. If only Enid knew how the girls at the factory went on: "What's happening now?" "The blinds down yet?" "How awful for you!" She drew up her knees, yawned, and crossed her arms on her breast. The young slip into the first attitude with beautiful ease and relaxation.

Because the house had been so quiet for days, the sound of a door bursting open, a chair scraped hurriedly back, shocked Marian out of sleep, and she lay trembling, her feet still entangled in the cardigan. She felt that it was about halfway through the night, but could not be sure. She heard Ron stumbling upstairs, tapping on her door. She put on her raincoat over her nightgown and went out to him.

"It's Gran," he said. "She's gone."

"What had I better do?" she asked in panic, with no example before her of how she should behave. He had wakened her but did not know why.

"Ron!" Enid came to the bottom of the stairs and called up. The light from the room behind her threw a faint nimbus around her head.

"Yes, Mother," he said, looking down at her.

"Did you wake Marian?"

"Yes." He answered guiltily, but evidently she thought his action right and proper.

"You will have to go for Mrs. Turner," his mother said.

"Why?"

"She—she's expecting you."

"In the middle of the night?"

"Yes. Right away—now." She turned away from the bottom of the stairs.

"Who is Mrs. Turner?" Marian whispered.

"I think—she lays people out." Ronny felt shame and uneasiness at his words, which seemed to him crude, obscene. The girl covered her face with her hands. "Oh, life's horrible."

"No, it's death, not life."

"Don't leave me."

"Come with me, then."

"Is it far?"

"No, not far. Hurry."

"Stand there by the door while I get ready."

Marian moved into the dark bedroom, and he stood leaning against the doorframe, waiting, with his arms folded across his chest. She came back quickly, wearing the raincoat, a scarf tied over her head.

They went downstairs into the bright kitchen, where Enid stood fixing candles into brass holders while her husband poured some brandy from an almost empty bottle into a glass. Enid drowned the brandy with warm water from the kettle and drank it off swiftly, her dark eyes expressionless.

"Give some to the children," she said, without thinking. They stiffened at the word "children" but took their brandy and water and sipped it.

"It's a cold night," said Enid. "Now go quickly."

"Marian's coming with me."

"So I see," said Enid. Her husband drank the last spoonful from the bottle, neat. "The end house, Lorne Street, right-hand side, by the Rose and Crown," she said, turning back to the other room.

The fumes of the brandy kindled in Ron's and Marian's breasts. "Remember that," he said. "The end house." He unlatched the back door.

"Next the Rose and Crown," she added. They slipped out into the beautiful, shocking air of the night.

When Ronny shone his torch down they could see the yellow hands of the leaves lying on the dark, wet pavements. Now there was only a flick of moisture in the air. He had taken her arm, and they walked alone in the streets, which flowed like black rivers. She wished that they might go on forever and never turn back towards that house. Or she would like it to be broad daylight, so that she could be at work, giggling about it all with the girls. ("Go on, Marian!" "How awful for you!")

His arm was pressed against her ribs. Sometimes she shivered from the cold and squeezed him to her. Down streets and around corners they went. Not far away goods trains shunted up and down. Once she stumbled over a curb, and in saving her he felt the sweet curve of her breast against his arm and walked gaily and with elation, filled with excitement and delight, swinging the beam of the torch from side to side, thinking it was the happiest evening of his life, seeing the future opening out suddenly like a fan, revealing all at once the wonder of human relationships.

"The Rose and Crown," she whispered. The building was shuttered for the night, the beer smells all washed away by the rain, the signboard creaking in the wind.

"The next house, then." She felt tensed up, but he was relaxed and confident.

"I've forgotten the name," she said.

"Turner."

They went up a short path onto a dark porch and knocked at the door. After a moment a window at the front of the house was thrown up and a woman's voice called out. They stepped back into the garden and looked up.

"Who is it?" the voice asked.

"We're from Mrs. Baker's," Ron said.

"Poor soul! She's gone, then, at last. How's your mother?"

Ronnie considered this and then said, "She's tired."

"She will be. Wait there, and I'll come along with you." She disappeared, and the window was slammed down.

"She seemed an ordinary sort of woman," whispered Marian.

They drew back into the shelter of the porch and waited. No sounds came from the house, but a smell of stuffiness seemed to drift out through the letter-slot in the door.

"Suppose she goes back to bed and leaves us here?" Marian asked and began to giggle. She put her mouth against his shoulder to stifle the little giggles, and he put his arm around her. She lifted her paper-white face in the darkness, and they kissed. The word "bliss" came into his mind, and he tasted it slowly on his tongue as if it were a sweet food. Platitudes began to come true for them, but they could not consider them as such.

Suddenly a step sounded on the other side of the door; bolts were slid back with difficulty; a chain rattled.

"Here we are!" said the brisk voice. The woman stepped out onto the porch, putting on a pair of fur gloves and looking up at the night sky and the flocks of curdy, scudding clouds. "It's a sad time," she said. "A very sad time for your poor mum and dad. Come on, then, lad, you lead the way. Quick, sharp!"

And now the footsteps of the three of them rang out metallically upon the paving stones as they walked between the dark and eyeless cliffs of the houses.

The Idea of Age

When I was a child people's ages did not matter; but age mattered. Against the serious idea of age I did not match the grown-ups I knew—who had all an ageless quality—though time unspun itself from year to year. Christmases lay far apart from one another, birthdays even farther; but that time was running on was shown in many ways. I "shot out" of my frocks, as my mother put it. By the time I was ten I had begun to discard things from my heart and to fasten my attention on certain people whose personalities affected me in a heady and delicious way.

Though the years drew me upwards at a great pace, as if they were full of a hurried, *growing* warmth, the seasons still held. Summers netted me in bliss endlessly. Winter did not promise spring. But when the spring came I felt that it was there forever. I had no dread that a few days would filch it from me, and in fact a few days were much when every day was endless.

In the summer holidays, when we went to the country, the spell of the long August days was coloured, intensified, by the fascinations of Mrs. Vivaldi. My first thought when we arrived at the guesthouse in Buckinghamshire was to look for some sign of *her* arrival—a garden hat hanging in the porch, or books from Mudie's. She came there, she made it clear, to rusticate (a word she herself used, which put a little flushed constraint upon the ladies who kept the guesthouse, who felt it to be derogatory); she came to rest from the demands of London; and she did seem to be always very tired.

I remember so many of the clothes she wore, for they seemed to me unusual and beautiful. A large hat of coarse Hessian sacking was surprisingly lined under the brim with gold lamé, which threw a light over her pale face. In the evenings panels heavy with steel-bead embroidery swung away from her as she walked. She was not content to appeal only to one's sight, with her floating scarves, her fringes and tassels, but made claims upon the other senses, with scents of carnations and jasmine, with the rustling of moiré petticoats and the more solid sound of heavy amber and ivory bracelets sliding together on her wrists. Once, when we were sitting in the garden on a still afternoon, she narrowed her hand and wriggled it out of the bracelets and tried them on me. They were warm and heavy, alive like flesh. I felt this to be one of the situations I would enjoy in retrospect but found unendurable at the time. Embarrassed, inadequate, I turned the bracelets on my arm; but she had closed her eyes in the sun.

I realize now that she was not very young. Her pretty ash-blond hair had begun to have less blond, more ash; her powdered-over face was lined. Then I did not think of her as being any age. I drifted after her about house and garden, beset by her magic, endeavouring to make my mark on her.

One evening in the drawing room she recited for the guests the Balcony Scene from *Romeo and Juliet*—all three parts—sitting on the end of the sofa, with her pearls laced through her fingers, her bronze shoes with pointed toes neatly together. Another evening, in that same room, she turned on the radio and fixed the headphones over my ears (pieces of sponge lessened the pressure), and very far off, through a tinkling, scuffling, crackling atmosphere, I heard Edith Sitwell reciting through a megaphone. Mrs. Vivaldi impressed me with the historical nature of the occasion. She made historical occasions seem very rare and to be fastened onto. Since then life has been one historical occasion after another, but I remember that scene clearly, and the lamplight in the room with all the beautiful china. The two ladies who kept the guesthouse had come down in the world and brought cupboards full of Crown Derby with them. The wireless set, with its coils and wires, was on a mosaic-topped table that, one day, my brother stumbled against and broke. It disintegrated almost into powder, and my mother wept. Mrs. Vivaldi walked with her in the garden. I saw them going under the rose-arches—the fair head and the dark—both very tall. I thought they looked like ladies in a book by Miss Braddon.

One afternoon I was alone in the drawing room when Mrs. Vivaldi came in from the garden with a basketful of sweet peas. As if the heat were suddenly too much for her, she sat down quite upright in a chair, with the basket beside her, and closed her eyes.

The room was cool and shadowy, with blinds half drawn to spare the threadbare carpet. The house seemed like a hollow shell; its subfusc life had flowed out into the garden, to the croquet lawn, to the shade of the mulberry tree, where elderly shapes sagged in deck chairs, half covered with newspapers.

I knew that Mrs. Vivaldi had not seen me. I was reading, sitting in my ungainly way on the floor, with my body slewed round so that my elbows and my book rested on the seat of a chair. Down there among the legs of furniture, I seemed only part of the overcrowded room. As I read I ate sweets out of a rather grubby paper bag. Nothing could, I felt, have been more peaceful than that afternoon. The clock ticked, sweets dissolved in my cheek. The scent of the flowers Mrs. Vivaldi had brought in began to mix with the clove smell of pinks outside. From the lawn came only an occasional grim word or two—the word "partner" most of all, in tones of exhortation or apology—and the solid sound of the mallet on the ball. The last smells of luncheon had faded, and the last distant clatter of washing-up. Alone in the room with Mrs. Vivaldi, I enjoyed the drowsy afternoon with every sense and also with peaceful feelings of devotion. I liked to be there while she slept. I had her presence without needing to make her love me, which was tiring.

Her presence must have been enough, for I remember that I sat with my back to her and only once or twice turned to glance in her direction. My book was about a large family of motherless children. I did not grudge children in books their mothers, but I did not want them to run the risk, which haunted me, of losing them. It was safer if their mother had already gone before the book began, and the wound healed, and I always tried to choose stories in which this had happened.

From time to time I glanced a little beyond the book and fell into reverie. I tried to imagine my own mother, who had gone out walking that afternoon, alone in the cherry orchard that ran down from hilltop to valley. Her restlessness often sent her off on long walks, too long for me to enjoy. I always lagged behind, thinking of my book, of the large, motherless family. In the cherry orchard it would be hot and scented, with bees scrambling into flowers and faded blue butterflies all over the chicory and heliotrope. But I found that I could not imagine her walking there alone; it seemed an incomplete picture that did not contain me. The reality was in this room, with its half-drawn blinds, its large gros-point picture of a cavalier saying good-bye to his lady. (Behind him a soldier said good-bye in a less affecting way to a servant.) The plush-covered chairs, the Sèvres urns were so familiar to me, so present, as never to fade. It was one of those stamped scenes, heeled down into my experience, which cannot link up with others or move forward or change. Like a dream, it was separate, inviolable, and could be preserved. Then I suddenly thought that I should not have let my mother go out alone. It was a revolutionary thought, suggesting that children have some protection to offer to grown-ups. I did not know from what I should have protected her—perhaps just from her lonely walk that hot afternoon. I felt an unwelcome stir of pity. Until now I had thought that being adult put one beyond the slur of being pitiable.

I tried to return to my book, to draw all those children round me for safety, but in my disturbed mind I began to feel that Mrs. Vivaldi was not asleep. A wasp zigzagged round the room and went abruptly, accidentally, out of the window. It did not leave the same peace behind, but unease. I could see myself—with *her* eyes—hunched up over my book, my frock crumpled under me, as I endlessly sorted out and chose and ate and brooded over my bag of sweets. I felt that I had intruded, and it was no longer a natural thing to be indoors on such a day. If she was awake I must get up and speak to her.

Her hand supported her head, her white elbow was on the plush arm of the chair. In that dark red chair she seemed very white and fair, and I could see long blue veins branching down the inside of her arm.

As I went towards her I saw, through the slats of her parted fingers, her lashes move. I stood in front of her, holding out the bag of sweets, but she did not stir. Yet so sure was I that she was awake that I did not know how to move away or leave her. Just as *my* hand wavered uncertainly *her* hand fell from her face. She opened her eyes and made a little movement of her mouth, too delicate to be called a yawn. She smiled. "I must have dropped off for a moment," she said. She glanced at the basket of flowers, at the clock, then at my bag of sweets.

"How kind of you!" she murmured, shaking her head, increasing my awkwardness. I took a few steps to one side, feeling I was looming over her.

"So you were here all the time?" she asked. "And I asleep. How dreadful I must have looked." She put her hand to the plaited hair at the nape of her neck. "Only young people should be seen asleep."

She was always underlining my youth, emphasizing her own age. I wanted to say, "You looked beautiful," but I felt clumsy and absurd. I smiled foolishly and wandered out into the garden, leaving my book in the room. The painted balls lay over the lawn. The syringa made the paths untidy with dropped blossom. Everyone's afternoon was going forward but mine. Interrupted, I did not know where to take it up. I began to wonder how old Mrs. Vivaldi was. Standing by the buddleia tree, I watched the drunken butterflies clinging to the flowers, staggering about the branches. Why did she pretend? I asked myself. I knew that children were not worth acting for. No one bothered to keep it up before us; the voices changed, the faces yielded. We were a worthless audience. That she should dissemble for me made me feel very sad and responsible. I was burdened with what I had not said to comfort her.

I hid there by the buddleia a long time, until I heard my mother coming up the path, back from her walk. I dreaded now more than ever that her step would drag, as sometimes it did, or that she would sigh. I came out half fearfully from behind the buddleia tree.

She was humming to herself, and when she saw me she handed me a large bunch of wild strawberries, the stalks warm from her hand. She sat down on the grass under the tree and, lifting her long arms, smoothed her hair, pressing in the hairpins more firmly. She said, "So you crept out of that stuffy little room after all?"

I ate the warm, gritty strawberries one by one, and my thoughts hovered all over her as the butterflies hovered over the tree. My shadow bent across her, as my love did.

The Light of Day

"And so she has borne you another son," said the doctor, raising his voice a little, as one who quotes the Bible. He sat sideways to their breakfast table to show that he was just off.

"Yes, we may use that word again," the father agreed. "It is odd that women do not *bear* their daughters, only have them."

Sitting in his wife's place, he began to pour out tea, and handed the cups clumsily so that they rocked in their saucers. Overhead floorboards creaked, and at intervals the newly born broke into paroxysms of despair as if he were being thrashed. Neither of the men seemed to hear this, sipping at their tea, passing their hands with a harsh sound across their unshaven chins.

The little maid brought in the children to their breakfast. They suffered the doctor's jocularity passively, used to it, for he was good with children. Their bibs were tied, milk poured.

"It is here," the boy said suddenly, pointing his spoon to the ceiling. "Crying like a real baby."

The girl listened, food at a standstill in her mouth. When her brother said those words, "It is here," the truth dawned in her and she understood that it had been necessary to make that point about its being a real baby because it had been an unreal one for so long. She came out of her daze, and excitement broke loose in her. Wrenching down her mouthful, she began to cry.

The young maid tried to comfort her, but she was flurried herself. This event she had so secretly dreaded was now over, and in her relief she could scarcely believe, after all the novels she had read, the stories she had heard, that the first thing to waken her had been that curious cry. "One of the children," her trained ear had warned her, the selective ear which had ignored the car arriving, the footsteps on the stairs, the doors opening and shutting. But the sound, so strident and protesting, was not from one of the peacefully sleeping children. It was the new one, the dreaded one. The little boy turned then and murmured in his sleep, flinging an arm across the pillow; but the girl sat up in bed and said, "There is a baby crying in this house," and listened, very still, the breeze from the window lifting her light hair up and back from her face.

"Another cup?" the father now asked the doctor.

"No, I'll be away. Cheer up, lass," he said, passing the little girl's chair, putting his hand on her head until she ducked away. "No tears today, you know," he added vaguely, and went on into the hall, where he looked round sleepily for his hat and his case.

Upstairs the baby was being bathed. Against the rush of

air on his body he had furiously protested; now he resisted the flow of water over his limbs. By the fire flannel, faintly scorched, waited for him.

"Then there'll be a nice cup of tea for you," the old nurse was saying, for it is all cups of tea when a baby is born.

The mother lay back drowsily, high on her pillows, feeling like a great battered boat washed up on the shore, empty, discarded. "Enjoy this moment," she told herself, "before life breaks over you again. Enjoy the soothing peace, the sloughed-off responsibilities, the handing over to others. A whole moment of bliss . . ."

You did well, she wanted someone to say, as if she were an actress on a first night. Soon flowers would begin to come, the husband's first, the six pink roses all lolling to one side of the wrong sort of vase.

I saw him born, almost, she thought. I propped myself up and watched him take his first breath, lying there, splayed out, mottled, veiled with a pearly film. His great chest arched up, his face darkened, the cry burst from him. "It is *vile* being born," he seemed to cry, the cold air leaping at him.

"When can the children come?" she asked drowsily.

"Not till he's bathed and dressed and you've had your tea. Plenty of time for them."

"But they want to see him *new*."

"He won't change much in half an hour."

But he was changed already—his folded mauve fists emerging from the frilled sleeve, his hair like damp feathers brushed up.

"There he is, then," cried the nurse, enchanted at her work.

There he was, frilled, featherstitched, and ribboned, rushed into the uniform of civilization, so quickly tamed, altered, made to conform. His head bobbed grotesquely, weakly, his lashless eyes turned to the light.

"And *there* he is," the nurse continued, "and there he *is*, then." And she twisted him in his shawl and laid him down beside his mother in the bed.

God, I'm so tired, the mother thought, bored. She forced her thumb into his fist, examined the little nails, stroked with the back of a finger the damp and silken hair, the tender cheek, breathed in the smell of him. Then her eyes drooped heavily, her body seemed dragged down backwards into sleep.

"You must take him away, nurse," she said. "Show him to the children. I'm—" She began to succumb to the heavy weight of sleepiness; but the nurse believed that mothers like to have their babies nestling beside them for a little while after they are born; the sight of this pleased her always and put the finishing touches to the birth, she thought.

Just as she was slipping away, down a fast stream of sleep, the door was tapped and the husband came in, shaved now and carrying tea.

"I am just off," he announced. "All is well downstairs."

Waking again, she suddenly asked, wailing a little, "But is it *really* well? And did they have their cod-liver oil?"

"Now, now," soothed the nurse, thinking of the milk.

"Yes, they had it," he said, and he bent over his new son with conventional clucking noises—making a fool of himself, they all thought. The baby began to cram tiny fingers into his mouth. The nurse stirred the tea, standing by.

The husband knew he was being dismissed. It was his third time of being a father. He bent over and kissed his wife. "You did well," he said, and she smiled peacefully, for nothing could hold her back now. She went swiftly—feet first, it seemed—sliding, falling, swimming, into darkness. Beside her, his mouth closing upon, then relinquishing his bent knuckles, the baby turned his eyes with a look of wonder to the light outside.

A Red-Letter Day

The hedgerow was beaded with silver. In the fog the leaves dripped with a deadly intensity, as if each falling drop were a drop of acid.

Through the mist cabs came suddenly face to face with one another, passing and repassing between station and school. Backing into the hedges—twigs, withered berries striking the windows—the drivers leaned out to exchange remarks, incomprehensible to their passengers, who felt oddly at their mercy. Town parents especially shrank from this malevolent landscape—wastes of rotting cabbages, flint cottages with rakish privies, rubbish heaps, grey napkins dropping on clotheslines, the soil like plum cake. Even turning in at the rather superior school gates, the mossy stone, the smell of fungus, still dismayed them. Then, as the building itself came into view, they could see Matron standing at the top of the steps, fantastically white, shaming nature, her hands laid affectionately upon the shoulders of such boys as could not resist her. The weather was put in its place. The day would take its course.

Tory was in one of the last of the cabs. Having no man to exert authority for her, she must merely take her turn, standing on the slimy pavement, waiting for a car to come back empty. She stamped her feet, feeling the damp creeping through her shoes. When she left home she had thought herself suitably dressed; even for such an early hour her hat was surely plain enough? One after another she had tried on, and had come out in the end leaving hats all over the bed, so that it resembled a new grave with its mound of wreathed flowers.

One other woman was on her own. Tory eyed her with distaste. Her sons (for surely she had more than one? She looked as if she had what is often called a teeming womb; was like a woman in a pageant symbolizing maternity), her many sons would never feel the lack of a father, for she was large enough to be both to them. Yes, Tory thought, she would have them out on the lawn, bowling at them by the hour, coach them at mathematics, oil their bats, dubbin their boots, tan their backsides (she was working herself up into a hatred of this woman, who seemed to be all that she herself was not)—one love affair in her life, or, rather, mating. "She has probably eaten her husband now that her childbearing days are over. He would never have dared to ask for a divorce, as mine did." She carried still her "mother's bag"—the vast thing which, full of napkins, bibs, bottles of orange juice, accompanies babies out to tea. Tory wondered what was in it now. Sensible things: a Bradshaw, ration books, a bag of biscuits, large clean handkerchiefs, a tablet of soap, and aspirins.

A jolly manner. "I love young people. I feed on them," Tory thought spitefully. The furs on her shoulders made her even larger; they clasped paws across her great authoritative back like hands across the ocean. Tory lifted her muff to hide her smile.

Nervous dread made her feel fretful and vicious. In *her* life all was frail, precarious; emotions fleeting, relationships fragmentary. Her life with her husband had suddenly loosened and dissolved, her love for her son was painful, shadowed by guilt—the guilt of having nothing solid to offer, of having grown up and forgotten, of adventuring still, away from her child, of not being able to resist those emotional adventures, the tenuous grasping after life; by the very look of her attracting those delicious secret glances, glimpses, whispers, the challenge, the excitement—not deeply sexual, for she was flirtatious; but not, she thought, watching the woman rearranging her furs on her shoulders, not a great feather-bed of oblivion. Between Edward and me there is no premise of love, none at all, nothing taken for granted as between most sons and mothers, but all tentative, agonized. We are indeed amateurs, both of us—no tradition behind us, no gift for the job. All we achieve is too hard come by. We try too piteously to please each other, and if we do, feel frightened by the miracle of it. I do indeed love him above all others. Above all others, but not exclusively.

Here a taxi swerved against the curb, palpitated as she stepped forward quickly, triumphantly, before Mrs. Hay-Hardy (whose name she did not yet know), and settled herself in the back.

"Could we share?" Mrs. Hay-Hardy asked, her voice confident, melodious, one foot definitely on the runningboard. Tory smiled and moved over much farther than was necessary, as if such a teeming womb could scarcely be accommodated on the seat beside her.

Shifting her furs on her shoulders, settling herself, Mrs. Hay-Hardy glanced out through the filming windows, undaunted by the weather, which would clear, she said, would lift. Oh, she was confident that it would lift by midday.

"One is up so early, it seems midday now," Tory complained.

But Mrs. Hay-Hardy had not risen until six, so that naturally it still seemed only eleven to her, as it was.

She will share the fare, Tory thought. Down to the last penny. There will be a loud and forthright women's argument. She will count out coppers and make a fuss.

This did happen. At the top of the steps Matron still waited with the three Hay-Hardys grouped about her, and Edward, who blushed and whitened alternately with terrible excitement, a little to one side.

To this wonderful customer, this profitable womb, the headmaster's wife herself came into the hall. Her husband had sent her, instructing her with deft cynicism from behind his detective novel, himself one of those gods who rarely descend, except, like Zeus, in a very private capacity.

This is the moment I marked off on the calendar, Edward thought. Here it is. Every night we threw one of our pebbles out of the window—a day gone. The little stones had dropped back onto the gravel under the window, quite lost, untraceable, the days of their lives.

As smooth as minnows were Mrs. Lancaster's phrases of welcome; she had soothed so many mothers, mothered so many boys. Her words swam all one way in unison, but her heart never moved. Matron was always nervous; the results of her work were so much on the surface, so checked over. The rest of the staff could hide their inefficiency or shift their responsibility; she could not. If Mrs. Hay-Hardy cried, "Dear boy, your teeth!" to her first-born, as she did now, it was Matron's work she criticized, and Matron flushed. And Mrs. Lancaster flushed for Matron; and Derrick Hay-Hardy flushed for his mother.

Perhaps I am not a born mother, Tory thought, going down the steps with Edward. They would walk back to the Crown for lunch, she said. Edward pressed her arm as the taxi, bulging with Hay-Hardys, went away again down the drive.

"Do you mean you wanted to go with them?" she asked.

"No."

"Don't you like them?"

"No."

"But why?"

"They don't like me."

Unbearable news for any mother, for surely all the world loves one's child, one's only child? Doubt set in, a little nagging toothache of doubt. You *are* happy? she wanted to ask. "I've looked forward so much to this," she said instead. "*So* much."

He stared ahead. All round the gateposts drops of moisture fell from one leaf to another; the stone griffins were hunched up in misery.

"But I imagined it being a different day," Tory added. "Quite different."

"It will be nice to get something different to eat," Edward said.

They walked down the road towards the Crown as if they

could not make any progress in their conversation until they had reached this point.

"You *are* warm enough at night?" Tory asked, when at last they were sitting in the hotel dining room. She could feel her question sliding away off him.

"Yes," he said absently and then, bringing himself back to the earlier, distant politeness, added, "Stifling hot."

"Stifling? But surely you have plenty of fresh air?"

"*I* do," he said reassuringly. "My bed's just under the window. Perishing. I have to keep my head under the bed-clothes or I get earache."

"I am asking for all this," she thought. When the waiter brought her pink gin she drank it quickly, conscious that Mrs. Hay-Hardy, across the hotel dining room, was pouring out a nice glass of water for herself. She was so full of jokes that Tory felt she had perhaps brought a collection of them along with her in her shopping bag. Laughter ran round and round their table above the glasses of water. Edward turned once, and she glimpsed the faintest quiver under one eye, and an answering quiver on the middle Hay-Hardy's face.

She felt exasperated. Cold had settled in her; her mouth, her heart too, felt stiff.

"What would you like to do after lunch?" she asked.

"We could look round the shops," Edward said, nibbling away at his bread as if to keep hunger at arm's length.

The shops were in the Market Square. At the draper's the hats were steadily coming round into fashion again. "I could astonish everyone with one of these," Tory thought, setting her own hat right by her reflection in the window.

Bales of apron-print rose on both sides; a wax-faced little boy wore a stiff suit, its price-ticket dangling from his yellow, broken fingers, his painted blue eyes turned mildly upon the street. Edward gave him a look of contempt and went to the shop door. Breathing on the glass in a little space among suspended bibs and jabots and parlourmaids' caps, he watched the cages flying overhead between cashier and counter.

The Hay-Hardys streamed by, heading for the open country.

Most minutely, Tory and Edward examined the draper's shop, the bicycle shop, the family grocer's. There was nothing to buy. They were just reading the postcards in the newsagent's window when Edward's best friend greeted them. His father, a clergyman, snatched off his hat and clapped it to his chest at the sight of Tory. When she turned back to the postcards she could see how unsuitable they were—jokes about bloomers, about twins; a great seaside world of fat men in striped bathing suits; enormous women trotted down to the sea's edge; crabs humorously nipped their behinds; farcical situations arose over bathing machines, and little boys had trouble with their water. She blushed.

The afternoon seemed to give a little sigh, stirred itself, and shook down a spattering of rain over the pavements. Beyond the Market Square the countryside, which had absorbed the Hay-Hardys, lowered at them.

"Is there anything you want?" Tory asked desperately, coveting the warm interiors of the shops.

"I could do with a new puncture outfit," Edward said.

They went back to the bicycle shop. My God, it's only three o'clock! Tory despaired, glancing secretly under her glove at her watch.

The Museum Room at the Guildhall was not gay, but at least there were Roman remains, a few instruments of torture, and half a mammoth's jawbone. Tory sat down on a seat among all the broken terra-cotta and took out a cigarette. Edward wandered away.

"No smoking, please," the attendant said, coming out from behind a case of stuffed deer.

"Oh, please!" Tory begged. She sat primly on the chair, her feet together, and when she looked up at him her violet eyes flashed with tears.

The attendant struck a match for her, and his hand, curving round it, trembled a little.

"It's the insurance," he apologized. "I'll have this later, if I may," and he put the cigarette she had given him very carefully in his breast pocket, as if it were a lock of her hair.

"Do you have to stay here all day long with these dull little broken jugs and things?" she asked, looking round.

He forgave her at once for belittling his life's work, only pointing out his pride, the fine mosaic on the wall.

"But floor should be lying down," she said naïvely—not innocently.

Edward came tiptoeing back.

"You see that quite delightful floor hanging up there?" she said. "This gentleman will tell you all about it. My son adores Greek mythology," she explained.

"Your son!" he repeated, affecting gallant disbelief, his glance stripping ten or fifteen years from her. "This happens to be a Byzantine mosaic," he said and looked reproachfully at it for not being what it could not be. Edward listened grudgingly. His mother had forced him into similar situations at other times: in the Armoury of the Tower of London; once at Kew. It was as if she kindled in men a little flicker of interest and admiration which her son must keep fanned, for she would not. Boredom drew her away again, yet her charm must still hold sway. So now Edward listened crossly to the story of the Byzantine mosaic, as he had last holidays minutely observed the chasing on Henry VIII's breastplate, and in utter exasperation the holidays before that watched curlews through fieldglasses ("Edward is so very keen on birds") for the whole of a hot day while Tory dozed elegantly in the heather.

Ordinary days perhaps are better, Edward thought. Sinking down through him were the lees of despair, which must at all costs be hidden from his mother. He glanced up at every clock they passed and wondered about his friends. Alone with his mother, he felt unsafe, wounded and wounding; saw himself in relation to the outside world, oppressed by responsibility. Thoughts of the future, and even, as they stood in the church porch to shelter from another little gust of rain, of death, seemed to alight on him, brushed him, disturbed him, as they would not do if he were at school, anonymous and safe.

Tory sat down on a seat and read a notice about missionaries, chafing her hands inside her muff while all her bracelets jingled softly.

Flapping, black, in his cassock, a clergyman came hurrying through the graveyard, between the dripping umbrella trees. Edward stepped guiltily outside the porch as if he had been trespassing.

"Good afternoon," the vicar said.

"Good afternoon," Tory replied. She looked up from blowing the fur of her muff into little divisions, and her smile broke warmly, beautifully, over the dark afternoon.

Then, "The weather—" both began ruefully, broke off and hesitated, then laughed at each other.

It was wonderful; now they would soon be saying good-bye. It was over. The day they had longed for was almost over—the polite little tea among the chintz, the wheel-back chairs of the Copper Kettle; Tory frosty and imperious with the waitresses, and once Edward beginning, "Father—" at which she looked up sharply before she could gather together the careful indifference she always assumed at this name. Edward faltered. "He sent me a parcel."

"How nice!" Tory said, laying ice all over his heart. Her cup was cracked. She called the waitress. She could not drink tea from riveted china, however prettily painted. The waitress went sulkily away. All round them sat other little boys with their parents. Tory's bracelets tinkled as she clasped her hands tightly together and leaned forward. "And how," she asked brightly, indifferently, "how is your father's wife?"

Now the taxi turned in at the school gates. Suddenly the day withdrew; there were lights in the ground-floor windows. She thought of going back in the train, a lonely evening. She would take a drink up to her bedroom and sip it while she did her hair, the gas fire roaring in its white ribs, Edward's photograph beside her bed.

The Hay-Hardys were unloading at the foot of the steps; flushed from their country walk and all their laughter, they seemed to swarm and shout.

Edward got out of the taxi and stood looking up at Tory, his new puncture outfit clasped tightly in his hand. Uncertainly, awaiting a cue from her, he tried to begin his good-bye.

Warm, musky-scented, softly rustling, with the sound of her bracelets, the touch of her fur, she leaned and kissed him. "So lovely, darling!" she murmured. She had no cue to give him. Mrs. Hay-Hardy had gone into the school to have a word with Matron, so she must find her own way of saying farewell.

They smiled gaily as if they were greeting each other.

"See you soon."

"Yes, see you soon."

"Good-bye, then, darling."

"Good-bye."

She slammed the door and, as the car moved off, leaned to the windows and waved. He stood there uncertainly, waving back, radiant with relief; then, as she disappeared round the curve of the drive, ran quickly up the steps to find his friends and safety.

The First Death of Her Life

Suddenly tears poured from her eyes. She rested her forehead against her mother's hand and let the tears soak into the counterpane.

Dear Mr. Wilcox, she began; for her mind was always composing letters. I shall not be at the shop for the next four days, as my mother has passed away and I shall not be available until after the funeral. My mother passed away very peacefully. . . .

The nurse came in. She took her patient's wrist for a moment, replaced it, removed a jar of forced lilac from beside the bed as if this were no longer necessary, and went out again.

The girl kneeling by the bed had looked up.

Dear Mr. Wilcox, she resumed, her face returning to the counterpane. My mother has died. I shall come back to work the day after tomorrow. Yours sincerely, Lucy Mayhew.

Her father was late. She imagined him hurrying from work, bicycling through the darkening streets, dogged, hunched up, slush thrown up by his wheels. Her mother did not move. She stroked her hand with its loose gold ring, the callused palms, the fine long fingers. Then she stood up stiffly, her knees bruised from the waxed floor, and went to the window.

Snowflakes turned idly, drifting down over the hospital gardens. It was four o'clock in the afternoon, and already the day seemed over. So few sounds came from this muffled and discoloured world. In the hospital itself there was a deep silence.

Her thoughts came to her in words, as if her mind spoke them first, understood them later. She tried to think of her childhood: little scenes she selected to prove how they had loved each other. Other scenes, especially last week's quarrel, she chose to forget, not knowing that in this moment she sent them away forever. Only loving-kindness remained.

But all the same, intolerable pictures broke through—her mother at the sink; her mother ironing; her mother standing between the lace curtains, staring out at the dreary street with a wounded look in her eyes; her mother tying the same lace curtains with yellow ribbons; attempts at lightness, gaicty, which came to nothing; her mother gathering her huge black cat to her, burying her face in its fur, and a great shivering sigh—of despair, of boredom—escaping her.

She no longer sighed. She lay very still and sometimes took a little sip of air. Her arms were neatly at her sides. Her eyes, which all day long had been turned to the white lilac, were closed. Her cheekbones rose sharply from her bruised, exhausted face. She smelled faintly of wine.

A small lilac flower floated on a glass of champagne, now discarded on the table at her side.

The champagne, with which they hoped to stretch out the thread of her life minute by minute; the lilac; the room of her own, coming to her at the end of a life of drabness and denial, just as, all along the mean street where they lived, the dying and the dead might claim a lifetime's savings from the bereaved.

She is no longer there, Lucy thought, standing beside the bed.

All day her mother had stared at the white lilac; now she had sunk away. Outside, beyond the hospital gardens, mist settled over the town, blurred the street lamps.

The nurse returned with the matron. Ready to be on her best behaviour, Lucy tautened. In her heart she trusted her mother to die without frightening her, and when the matron, deftly drawing Lucy's head to rest on her own shoulder, said in her calm voice, "She has gone," she felt she had met this happening halfway.

A little bustle began, quick footsteps along the empty passages, and for a moment she was left alone with her dead mother. She laid her hand timidly on her soft dark hair, so often touched, played with when she was a little girl, standing on a stool behind her mother's chair while she sewed.

There was still the smell of wine and the hospital smell. It was growing dark in the room. She went to the dressing table and took her mother's handbag, very worn and shiny, and a book, a library book which she had chosen carefully for her, believing she would read it.

Then she had a quick sip from the glass on the table, a mouthful of champagne, which she had never tasted before, and, looking wounded and aloof, walked down the middle of the corridor, feeling the nurses falling away to left and right.

Opening the glass doors onto the snowy gardens, she thought that it was like the end of a film. But no music rose up and engulfed her. Instead there was her father turning in at the gates. He propped his bicycle against the wall and began to run clumsily across the wet gravel.

Shadows of the World

"I don't call this the real country," she said. "People only *sleep* here."

From the window she watched the cars going by from the station. There was almost a stream of traffic, for the London train was in.

"And not always with whom they should," George Eliot agreed. His name was something he had to carry off. He tried to be the first with the jokes and never showed his weariness. His parents were the most unliterary people and had chosen his name because it had somehow sprung to their minds, sounding right and familiar. Taking that in his stride had originated his flamboyance, his separateness. He made his mark in many dubious ways; but the ways *were* only dubious and sometimes he was given the benefit of the doubt. As a bachelor, he was a standby to dissatisfied wives, and only the wives knew—and would not say—how inadequate he turned out to be.

"There go the Fletchers," Ida said. "What a mass of

silverware they have on that car! They were sitting bolt upright and not speaking to each other."

"How could you see? She would scarcely have her head on his shoulder just driving back from the station."

"Nor on any other occasion. Nor his on hers."

"Come away from the window and talk to me. What time will Leonard come?"

"Who could know but Leonard? He might have caught that train and stepped aside on the way."

"For a drink?"

"It might be that even," she said, brightly insinuating. She turned her back to the window, but stayed where she was. The branches of trees with their young leaves came close to the house and threw a greenish shadow over the walls inside. The colours of the spring evening were intense rather than brilliant: the lilac was heaped up against sky of the same purple. A house nearby had a sharp outline, as if before rain; but there had been neither rain nor sun for several days. Swallows flew low so that she could see their pale, neat bellies as they flickered about the eaves. In the wood cuckoos answered one another at long intervals, haltingly; one had its summer stammer already—its explosive, broken cry.

"The peonies almost open! How it all hastens by and vanishes!" Ida said, working herself up for a storm of her own.

"Why not have a drink?" George asked. He had come in for that, and because it looked like being a dark and thundery evening. No golf.

"I hate our lives," she cried. "We fritter our time away." She looked round the room, at the rather grubby rough-cast walls, little pictures hanging crooked, the red-brick fireplace with its littered grate, its dusty logs. Everything goes wrong with what I do, she thought. This room has simply no character. It looks raw, bleak, dull. When she studied pictures in magazines it all seemed easy enough, but her colour schemes became confused, something always obtruded. If she followed elaborate recipes what resulted was nothing like the photograph in the cookery book. Her enthusiasms scarcely deserved the name. Her piano-playing, to which she resorted in boredom, remained sketchy and improvised in the bass. Resolutions, too, soon abated. Slimming exercises, diets, taking the children to church, were all abandoned. Only dull habit remained, she thought. When her daughter wished to learn to play the violin, she refused. "You will want to give it up after a couple of lessons. You will never practise," she said, thinking only of her experience of herself; for Virginia was a tenacious child.

"A drink—?" George began once more. Though they were old friends he did not feel like going to what she called the cocktail cabinet and helping himself.

"I have nothing," she said moodily and dramatically. He looked surprised and alarmed. "The empty days," she continued, to his great relief, "the long, empty days."

"Oh, hell, I thought for one moment you meant the drink situation."

"Have what you want," she said ungraciously, impatiently.

"Those damn cuckoos!" He laughed, pausing with the bottle in his hand pointing at her like a gun, his head on one side.

She persisted in her mood, pacing the room, trying to

claim his whole attention. Vexed, frustrated, she was balked by his indifference.

"You have the children," he said. "This nice home." He glanced at the crooked pictures, at some fallen petals lying round a jar of flowers.

As if he were a conjurer, the door opened and Virginia came in. She looked like a Japanese doll, with her white face, her straight black hair with the curved fringe, and her brightly patterned frock. At the back of the house life was gayer. In the maid's sitting room she and the nineteen-year-old girl from the village gossiped and giggled. She held the edges of the sheets to the sewing machine while Nancy turned the handle, putting sides to middle. ("All the sheets are going at once," Ida had said bitterly, as if even household linen conspired against her.) The whir of the sewing machine interrupted their discussions, and they sucked sweets instead. The stuffy room smelled of pear-drops. But at seven Nancy said, "Hey, you! Go on. Bed. Hop it."

"Where's Laurie?"

"Out in the shed, I daresay, with the cat. You can just run quick and see whether there's any kittens yet, but mind, when I say 'quick' I don't mean your usual hanging about."

Virginia pressed her elbows to her sides. The oppressive evening menaced her with thunder and lightning, now with the horror of birth. Her mother had special feelings of the same kind—could forecast storms by her headaches; was sick at the smell of lilies; could not eat shellfish; and fainted at the sight of blood. She overreacted to the common things of life, even in physical ways, with giddiness and rashes on her skin. She taught her family to reverence her allergies and foibles, and they were constantly discussed.

"I don't want to go," Virginia had said.

"Then say good night to your mother," Nancy said as if she had no better alternative to offer.

Virginia did not want that either but stood obediently at the door, with her suspicious, upward look at them, at George and Ida.

Out in the shed Laurie hung over the cat's basket, absorbed, though a little frightened. His cat, Moira, swaying with her weight of kittens, trampled the basket, crying. When Laurie stroked her head she stopped, turning her golden eyes on him, appeased. She seemed as nervous as he, and as uninstructed. Maternity wrought an immediate, almost a comical change in her. The first kitten was born, silent, still. Laurie feared that it was dead. It looked so unkittenish—livid, slimed-over, more blue than black. But at once, Moira became definite and authoritative. She licked and cuffed, knocked the poor clambering thing—with its trailing navel-cord, its mouth pursed up like a flower bud—against the side of the basket. Fantastic, at last alive, it tried to lift on its stringy neck the nodding weight of its head. Its paws were more hands than paws, with frail claws outstretched, and piteously it raked the air with them.

Laurie imagined the edged cold after the warm, the discomforts of breathing. Surely, he thought, the poor creature felt, if not through its sealed eyes, then through its shivering body, the harsh, belabouring light, after such utter darkness.

Moira was arrogant in maternity; no uncertainty beset her now. When the kitten was cleaned she lay down on her side, awaiting the others, purring a little. She seemed contemptuous of Laurie now and gave him only an occasional, unseeing glance. At the approach of each birth she seemed to gather herself up, took on a suspicious look, with eyes narrowed. When she had cleaned them, the kittens were indistinguishable from her own black body, her thrust-out satiny legs. They clambered feebly over the mound of her belly even before the last was born; their pink hands frailly felt the air; splayed out on dampish legs, they looked old and burdened creatures; they mewed wretchedly, resenting the bitter, cuffing, hard-edged world in which they were—the unrocking, unyielding stubbornness of it. Black like their mother, they had bare-looking patches which would one day, Laurie thought, be white feet, white bibs. He looked forward for them. They peopled his home. He thought of them opening their eyes at last and playing; putting on mock terror at the sound of a footfall; arching their spines, cavorting, curvetting about the legs of the furniture.

The stream of cars had dwindled and run out. The beech leaves against the sloe-coloured sky looked more lucent; the birds' song, which had suddenly increased in urgency and hysteria, as suddenly ceased. Only a single thrush went on, and its notes echoed in the silence; the intent air vibrated with the sound.

Thirty miles from London, the village had a preponderance of middle-sized houses. They lay at the end of short but curving drives, embowered in flowering trees. At this time of the year the landscape was clotted with greenish creamy blossom—pear, white lilac, guelder-rose. Later, as it all faded, a faint grubbiness, a litter of petals seemed a total collapse. But there always were a great many birds: green woodpeckers appeared on the suburban-looking lawns; owls cried in the night. When the rain came it fell through layers of leaves, loosening gravel, staining the white rough-cast houses and vibrating on sunporches and greenhouses.

Ida was unusually placed in being able to see the road. Only rather low beech hedges separated her. The cars reminded her of fish going by in shoals. At the weekends when there were parties she would stand waiting by the window to be sure that plenty of her friends had gone by, not caring to be early. Like shoals of fish, they all headed one way, arrived at one destination (where there would be plenty to drink), turned homewards at last in unison.

Ida drank little, although sometimes at parties, because of her very indifference, she would accept glasses haphazardly with no knowledge of her mounting foolishness. She scorned and resented the way her acquaintances revolved round, took their pattern from, so much alcohol. For one thing, the cost dismayed her. She loved clothes, or rather new clothes, and her own clothes. It seemed that dozens of bottles of gin stood between her and all the things she wanted. George, who knew her so well, had no idea of her ill will each time he filled his glass, which he did while she was saying good night to Virginia.

Sounds of knives and forks being put out came from the dining room. Virginia, opening the door, had let in a steaminess from the kitchen, a smell of mint.

"Ask Nancy not to *race* the potatoes like that," Ida said. "Good night, darling one." She drew the child to her as if she were a springing young tree; Virginia leaned, but did not move her feet. Her mother used endearments a great deal—

sometimes to put an edge to displeasure. "*Darling*, how *could* you be so stupid!"

"I don't know if I should wait dinner for Leonard," she said to George, who was just raising his replenished glass. "You'll stay, won't you?"

"Well, I will, then. Do you mean Leonard just may not come home?"

She had a desire to lay waste something, if only George's complacency. "He may not come home to *me*."

"Then, dear, you are wondrous cool. Where else should he go?"

"To Isabel's, I expect."

"Isabel?"

"Oh, you must know," she said impatiently, surprised at her own tone.

"At the Fletchers' party, you mean? But parties are nothing. Everyone forgets the next day."

"Do they?"

She went to the window again, rapping her fingernails on the glass. She felt isolated because she did not forget the next day. Her own romantic hopes remained, and the young man at the party who had said, "You don't belong," and pressed his knuckles steadily against her thigh as they stood on the porch waiting for cars, who promised—so falsely—to seek her out again, was real to her; her brooding mood enlarged, improved him. She had taken no heed of Leonard all that evening, given no thoughts to him. But some impression had been formed, as if her mind had photographed, without her knowledge, the picture of Leonard and Isabel intently and obliviously talking. Now her dissatisfaction printed the negative. What had been to her advantage that evening suddenly infuriated her.

"I'm sure it's nothing," George assured her. "Your imagination. Just one of those village things."

She had imagined the young man sitting in this room with her. The fire was lit; flames had consumed the cigarette ends and litter. The house was silent, the walls receded into shadow. They watched the fire. . . .

"I thought I heard thunder," George said, hoping to turn the conversation, and also quietly, one-handedly, filling his glass.

"I feel it in my head," Ida said, putting her hand across her eyes. When she heard footsteps on the road she could not resist looking out again. She felt like the Lady of Shalott. "Shadows of the world appear," she thought. She imagined the young man, riding down between the hedges. But it was Isabel, going along the road in her old tweed coat with her dejected spaniel on a lead.

Virginia took off her vest and hung it over the mirror. Her nail scissors and a silver comb she put in a drawer away from the lightning. Naked, she was thin and long-legged, her side marked with a neat appendix scar. Her spine was silky, downy. She dropped her nightgown over her head and stood, legs apart, elbows up like wings, trying to do up buttons at the back.

Outside the sky seemed to congeal cruelly, charged with lead. At the first sound of thunder splitting across the roof she jumped into bed and lay under the thin coverings, quite rigid, as if she were dead.

The birth of the fourth, the last kitten, was a triumph. Creamy and blond tortoiseshell, it was distinguished and mysterious from the beginning, suggesting an elegant grandparent on one side or the other. Larger than the others, longer-haired, somehow complete at once, blind but not helpless, it put the finishing touches to the basket, decorated Moira's maternity.

Laurie shifted from his squatting position, feeling stiff, the pattern of wickerwork dented into one knee. He was relieved and exhilarated. Leaving benign, smug Moira, he went to put his bicycle away, for a few spots of rain had fallen on the path.

"Well, we won't wait," Ida said. The sight of Isabel had strangely frustrated her. "I'll tell Nancy, and Laurie must go to bed." She thought, Better to dine alone with George than have him drinking all this gin.

"Where *is* Laurie?"

"With his cat. She's having kittens."

She put her hand on the bell and when Nancy came gave orders for dinner to be served. "And tell Laurie it's bedtime."

"Four kittens," Nancy said. "Isn't that lovely?"

"Thank you, Nancy," Ida said in her quelling way.

"Whatever will you do with them?" George asked. "Four kittens."

"Do? What do you imagine? Need we go into details?"

The rain, suddenly released, fell like knives into the flowerbeds, bounced and danced on the paths. Different scents steamed up from the earth; the drenched lilac looked as if it would topple over with the weight of its saturated blossom.

Just as Nancy announced, with her touch of sarcasm, that dinner was served, Leonard's car swept into the drive. They heard him slamming the garage doors together. George drained his glass and put it reluctantly on the table. Leonard came running up from the garage, his head down and his shoulders stained dark with the rain.

Swan-Moving

The village stood high in scarred and quarried country. The hillside had been broken into in many places, and some of the wounds, untended, were covered with coarse weeds. Other English villages, with a good foundation of thatched cottages and leafy lanes, improve on their conscious beauty with loving care. Grass verges are shaved neatly, flowers overhang walls, and fruit trees, lime-washed to their chins, stand in orchards full of daffodils. This village lacked even the knowledge of its own ugliness, and nothing was done consciously in any direction. Gardens, in which scarcely a blade of grass remained, were littered with chicken droppings and feathers. On the common, round which the cottages stood, pieces of old bicycles rusted among nettles. Tin cans floated in the muddy water which filled—in wintertime—the deep hollows. In one an iron bedstead was half submerged. On this, the biggest pond, a swan was found one morning, circling disconsolately among the rubbish.

Nights for a long time had been muffled with fog. By mid-afternoon, the sky would have begun to congeal in a phlegmy discoloration, and then the village was cut off and abandoned to its own squalor.

The swan, arriving unseen, stayed so until late in the morning, when the fog shifted and began to roll down the hillside, leaving the crown of the hill standing in an uncertain light. Children coming out to play on the common saw what their fathers bicycling to work at the brick kilns could not have seen. They crowded the edge of the pond, and one boy threw a stick at the swan, trying to make him fly. That was the first and last unkindness the bird ever suffered in the village. The children discovered that more response came when food was thrown, and soon the pond and the trodden grass around were littered with crusts of bread and bacon rinds, orange peel and apple cores. Even in its charity, the village was backward and untidy, yet the swan, coming to it out of the fog and remaining as he did, stirred its imagination and pride. On the market bus and in the pub and post office he was the subject of conjecture and theory. Whence had he flown? they wondered—in what direction? Was he maimed and unable to fly any farther? Flattered as they were, the villagers could not believe that the muddy pond had ever been his true objective, heart's desire. They talked about the swan and worried over him. The vicar referred to him in his sermon on "The Mysterious Ways of the Lord."

After a week or two—the swan still circling on his muddy pond—strangers were seen about the village, which was becoming a popular diversion from the ennui of the Sunday walk. Mrs. Wheatley, at the Stag and Hounds, began to serve afternoon teas. Her son and some of his workmates removed the rusting bedstead from the pond and threw it into a bluebell wood. Eyes so lông indifferent became critical, and much was suddenly seen to be wrong. A committee was formed to put the common in order and was given its title—the Local Amenities Enhancement Council—by the vicar, who had a gift for words. To encourage beauty, a prize was offered for the neatest cottage garden, and a notice board was set up beside the pond with the words "Rubbish Prohibited."

It was the first time that the village had worked together on any project. The swan, the unacknowledged instigator, took all for granted, seemed indifferent to amenities, but grew noticeably less aloof, for now he would wait at the edge of the common for the children to come from school. Fussy over his food, he would peck about and reject most of it. His first meal of the day was at half-past six, when the men bicycled off to work. They would throw pieces from their "slicers," or lunch packets. Later the children, going to school, showered down all the crusts they had had no need for at breakfast, but the swan trod amongst them at the water's edge or avoided them as they floated on the pond.

Wet weather, dark days did not suit his looks. Not quite fully grown, he still had some of his dark plumage, and this was stained by the orange clay in the water. Standing forlornly and unsteadily in the mud, he seemed stiff with misery and perhaps rheumatism.

"Old chap looks rough," the men would say anxiously, coming from work. When strangers arrived on those days and appeared amused or made disparaging remarks, the children suffered painful indignation—a foretaste of parenthood.

But as the spring came and the wild cherry blossomed above the quarries, the swan began to dazzle with the same white brilliance. The flowers grew in the cottage gardens. They did not blossom well from so stamped-down and untended a soil, but a few wallflowers of a ghastly yellow were bedded out. Handwritten notices swung on gates and fences, announcing "Lemonade—a Penny per Glass" or "Cut Flowers—Sixpence the Bunch."

The swan, preening himself daily into greater beauty, was in himself a lesson, an example in seemliness, and the village began to preen and trim itself too, but with neither the habit of grace nor aptitude for it. Fair weather throughout that spring encouraged a refurbishing, a hurried business with buckets of whitewash and pots of paint. This fermenting creativeness had strange results. So many white curtains were taken down to appear later on clotheslines a dull but curious green or indigo or raspberry. Garments—even underclothes —of the same color hung beside them, for a bowl of dye is usually a great temptation. Few of the experiments were an improvement, and most of the villagers, in their new self-consciousness, went too far; yet, insidiously, the idea of charm spread through the village. A guilty tawdriness was its expression, naïve and peasant-like, but here without steadying ritual or tradition. The vicar, having once despaired at apathy, now winced at exuberance—at red-white-and-blue rabbit hutches, the new neon lighting outside the Stag and Hounds, and one of his sidesmen wearing a daffodil in his buttonhole at Evensong. He tried to control the general mood of recklessness, but the infection was at its height and beyond him.

In the midst of the wonderful weather, and because of it, the villagers could not avoid the knowledge that there had been summers—especially after such a spring—when the water in the pond had dwindled and gone, leaving a patch of cracked earth and rusty tins. Already it seemed to have receded, and nightly inspection of its level took place—a grave ceremony, like the inspection of a wicket, and confined to the men. They would report back to their women, and the news spread among the children—the water was down a quarter of an inch perhaps, or more, or seemed to remain the same. They all watched the sky for rain.

By the beginning of June, when the swan had been with them for nearly six months, the water had fallen so low that a meeting was called. When it was over, the men went off on their bicycles to look for better accommodation for the swan, who seemed too negligent to do so for himself.

The nearest stretch of water was over a mile away—a deep, clear pond in a buttercup field. Having inspected it, the men went home, and the next evening a great crowd came out on the common to watch the swan-moving.

The vicar drove up in his little car, which he left on the road, and walked down to the water's edge in his shirt sleeves. He wore his clerical collar and an old baize apron that he had borrowed from his manservant. The swan was coaxed out of the water with pieces of spongecake. The men moved forward slowly, the vicar motioning them in to form a half-circle. Very gently and in silence, they closed in on the swan. At this moment of great tension Mrs. Wheatley from the Stag and Hounds—an unstable woman—suddenly screamed and was shushed and nudged by her neighbours.

The vicar gathered up the swan against his apron and held him tenderly in his arms. In a most graceful and affectionate movement, the bird curved his shining neck against the vicar's shoulder. His lower feathers, his spread webbed feet, dripped dirty water as he was carried up the bank towards the car, the crowd surging after.

The swan sat on the front seat beside the vicar, and the manservant sat behind. When they drove away the crowd waved and cheered as if seeing off bride and bridegroom. The swan surveyed them with indifference. His feet were splayed out in an ungainly way on a piece of sacking, and as the car moved forward he crooked his neck and began to cleanse from his plumage the trace of human hands.

Men leaped onto their bicycles with their children across the bars or perched behind. The vicar drove slowly, and the procession went away down the side of the common, past the Stag and Hounds, where the bar had been left entirely in the hands of the village dipsomaniac, who had strange visions of his own and was not tempted from his vocation by such a happening, but he had the decency, long remembered to his credit, to come out and lift his glass as they all went by.

They streamed on between high hedges and ditches full of cow parsley and Queen Anne's lace, the swan now turning his head, his beak parting and closing as if he were thirsty or afraid. The vicar watched the road, and the manservant watched the swan. The bicyclists kept up—a noisy throng. Some had bunches of buttercups pinned to their caps. When the car was slowed up by cows crossing the road, the bicyclists came up to the car window and looked in approvingly.

"Sits up in the manner born," one said with pride.

When they moved on down the lane, which was steaming and smelling strongly of cowpats, the swan began to lurch about unsteadily. He turned his head and gave the vicar a long and strange glance, and the manservant leaned forward protectively. Then the beak sank into the great, rounded breast, and the eyes were covered, as if he slept.

The vicar stopped the car at the field gate and stepped out to face the throng, his hand raised high. "I want all done in silence now," he said. "Nothing to confuse him, so stand afar off." So important was the occasion that he fell easily into Biblical oratory and might have added "all of ye" without knowing or its being noticed.

They stood afar off among the polished grasses. It was an evening of great peace. The shadows were long ovals under the elm trees. Cows moved slowly through the yellow fields, and the water of the pond, still as a glass, reflected a mackerel sky.

The vicar and the manservant lifted the swan from his seat in the car and carried him to the edge of the pond, where they put him tenderly to the breast of the water, then stood aside.

It was a moment of great emotion, like the launching of a ship. The bird took to the pond and became two swans. In this clear water his reflection could be seen for the first time, and his foolish-looking feet paddling along. "Look!" cried a little boy, and his father put a hand over his mouth to silence him.

The swan went forward in great majesty, as if at last conscious of his true nature, and his wake spread out and followed like a train.

The vicar lifted his hand for a second and then touched his eyes. As he came back up the bank, his shoes wet and his baize apron plastered with clay, his parishioners—if such most of them could be called from the fact of living in the same parish—looked at him with respect. He had appeared to them a natural leader, a man of courage and decision.

They returned to the village and crowded into the Stag and Hounds. Some of them took their beer outside and looked over the common to the empty pond. Their lives had been touched so lightly by magic that perhaps only the seeds of a legend were left, or less—no trace at all—but they felt easeful, thinking of the swan in his new home. The vicar, who would have been an embarrassed man in the Stag and Hounds, and no longer a leader, went home and began to prepare his sermon, "Cast Thy Bread upon the Waters."

The swan, when they had all gone, swam about for a while, plunging his beak deep into the water and ruffling his feathers. Then he came to the pond's edge and out of the water. He stood there preening himself, a heraldic swan with wings half lifted. At last, with a tottering run, clumsy, seeming off balance with his huge breastbone thrust forward and his neck outstretched, he made a great commotion with his wings and took to the air. As he rose level with the setting sun his feathers were golden. Then he went higher and became a grey shape. The scent of far-off water came to him, and he flew on, away from that countryside forever.